LARAMIE NELSON RIDES AGAIN!

In Zane Grey's *Raiders of the Spanish Peaks,* Laramie Nelson, foreman of the Spanish Peaks Ranch, saved the Lindsay family from ruin, and settled down with the beautiful Hallie Lindsay and a respected position in the community.

But Laramie Nelson was not a man to stay put for long. In this volume, the lightning fast gunman is back on the trail, ready to cut down any trouble to cross his path.

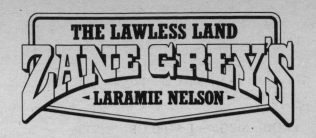

THE LAWLESS LAND

ZANE GREY'S

LARAMIE NELSON

ROMER ZANE GREY

LEISURE BOOKS   NEW YORK CITY

A LEISURE BOOK®

January 1990

Published by

Dorchester Publishing Co., Inc.
276 Fifth Avenue
New York, NY 10001

THE LAWLESS LAND

I

The startled upward flight of quail from the wooded north ridge was the first ominous warning.

No man with savvy, and Laramie Nelson had plenty of that, along with the usual healthy desire to stay alive and kicking a few more years, liked having a ridge rider stalking his trail.

From ingrained habit as a manhunter, his intent gray eyes had kept flicking right and left as he pushed west through the narrow valley. So he'd noticed the birds, obviously frightened by something—or someone. And as he looked again, he caught the flash of a white tail, a deer taking off fast.

Tall and spare, Laramie's sandy hair was sweated under his battered Stetson. And now beads of perspiration slowly trickled down his bronzed cheeks.

Under him was Wingfoot, his fine horse. Laramie slowed a bit, whipcord body easy in the high-pronged

9

saddle. He felt for his repeating carbine in the boot under a long, cocked leg, and made sure his Colt .45 revolver was slipping easily in its holster. He wore stained Levi's tucked into halfboots with high heels; he reached in a breast pocket of his shirt for the makings, made a cigarette with one hand, found a match and lit up, figuring what to do next.

He kept one eye on the ridge and finally glimpsed the crown of a black Stetson. The rider was right with him.

To the left was a shallow creek. If he kept heading west, Nelson could see he'd be forced into a constricted gap, where the stream broke through the hills. These were called hills, but anyone who hadn't seen the majestic Rockies and the high Sierras would have said they were mountains. Pine, cedar and other trees grew from the slopes, chaparral thick in the gaps, redstone outcrops thrusting up here and there.

Rough country. And tough, maybe tougher than any part of the great West. Laramie Nelson had worked in about every other area. The Nations, as Indian Territory was called, had become the hideout for every killer, horsethief and other assorted outlaws who could disappear into its comparative safety. There was no local law whatsoever, only loose federal jurisdiction administered from Fort Smith on the other side of the river.

"Nobody," muttered Laramie, as Wingfoot pricked up his velvet ears, "nobody but Brock Peters would send a lone Pinkerton into this cussed death trap!"

He slowed Wingfoot even more, feigning to relight the quirly, really figuring what he should do. With his carbine and sixgun he could put up a good fight, if it came down to that. Maybe he could beat the ridge rider to it—or maybe he couldn't. It would depend.

Bitterly, Nelson thought of Brock Peters; he could picture his boss's cherubic face as he gave Laramie orders back in Fort Smith. Peters was short and he dressed like a dude, but actually he was a top Pinkerton, which was why he held his high position.

Brock's headquarters were based in Denver, Colorado, but this operation had been considered so important, he'd been sent over to Arkansas, taking Laramie with him. Peters had rented a small house on a side street in Fort Smith as his base in the region. He intended to wait around the settlement for Laramie's report, except for quick trips to Van Buren and Little Rock.

Fort Smith was Judge Isaac C. Parker's bailiwick. Parker was the only federal magistrate within many miles, and he was stern and he had no mercy for lawbreakers. Outside the jail and courtroom stood a gallows on which a dozen men could be dropped at the same time. And if need be, Judge Parker would do that.

Deputy federal marshals would cross into the Nations on the trail of the most savage outlaws in the United States. The pay was low, so low you'd wonder why a man would take the job. In some years, half of the officers were shot down from ambush by the feral characters they hunted. A killer or notorious criminal preferred to shoot it out and chance dying with his boots on rather than face Judge Parker and his hanging machine.

And still the federal marshals rode into the Territory in search of their prey, human prey far more dangerous than any wild animal.

"Yeah," Brock Peters had said, somewhat tactlessly it had seemed to Laramie, "four Pinkertons have already been killed on this job. That's why I offered to put *you* on it."

11

"Offered me as a human sacrifice?"

Peters frowned. "Never mind the jokes, Nelson. We're supposed to protect the Butterfield stage line that runs through Fort Smith, and other folks Pinkerton has contracts with. Why, every other stage has been robbed of money shipments, passengers gun-whipped and their valuables taken. A few young women have been carried off. The stage line threatens to cancel our contract and hire a rival outfit to protect 'em if Pinkerton can't!"

Laramie set Wingfoot ahead but the closer he drew to that gap, the less he liked it. The walls were perpendicular red rock, the trail skirting the creek. Anyone on the bluffs could shoot a rider below without exposing himself.

He killed his cigarette, whirled Wingfoot, and galloped back the way he'd come, meaning to locate another route west.

Then he saw the horsebacker coming at him with a carbine at the ready across his pommel. Laramie stopped Wingfoot so fast the horse's hoofs slid.

He snatched his rifle from its boot and threw a couple over the horsebacker, who veered, zigzagged, and fired back. The slugs buzzed too close for anybody's health, and the man sang out but Laramie didn't wait to hear his arguments.

Splashing across the creek, he set Wingfoot up the steep, bushy south slope at an angle. The horsebacker let go again, and shale kicked up close to the moving horse.

Laramie reached an outcropping which offered some protection, and paused. He jumped down; Wingfoot couldn't climb fast on such a scarp, and Nelson feared the pursuer might shoot his mount.

He swung and raised his carbine. The horsebacker had

12

stopped, slid off his saddle, and stood behind his horse. Laramie could see the man watching him, and if Laramie pulled trigger, the fellow would duck down and shoot with a good chance of hitting Nelson, or Wingfoot.

Shots echoed from across the valley. The ridge rider had appeared and was shouting and firing as he shoved down to join the horsebacker who'd blocked Laramie from retreating.

Puffing a bit, Nelson dug in his high heels and heaved up the hill, dragging Wingfoot after him.

He'd almost made it—he thought.

Then he had a funny feeling. He didn't know why, but he had it, and just as he reached the south rim, he found out. Two more were waiting for him.

They jumped out, guns up, covering him from either side. The stern-faced hombres were alert; one stocky fellow gripped a choke-barrel shotgun aimed at Laramie, the second, leaner and nastier looking, held a Winchester carbine ready to fire.

"Drop it," snapped the lean one coldly, "and put up the paws. One wrong move, you're dead!"

"Yessir, I can see that." Nelson let his rifle fall and reached.

"Tie his hands behind him, Murphy, throw his rope around his craw. Choke him if he balks." That was the lean one.

"Okay, Rollins. Here comes Ince. Morris is on the way."

The horsebacker moved up to join the jolly party. Rollins seemed to be chief. Ince arrived, grim, heavily armed. "Good, got him without any of us bein' shot," congratulated Rollins. He pulled out a cheroot and

13

calmly lit up. They waited for Morris, who finally came up. Morris had a fleshy face which somehow reminded Laramie of Brock Peters.

"All right, boys," said Rollins. "Let's add this one to the collection."

Ince jerked on the lasso and the noose cut Laramie's neck. Morris led Wingfoot behind.

None of them were old. Rollins might have been in his early thirties but the others looked younger.

Suddenly Laramie Nelson noticed the tarnished badges pinned under the flapping lapels of their breast pockets.

He'd kept quiet because he didn't know who or what they might be. Now relief flooded him. "Say, you boys must be deputy marshals, Judge Parker's officers."

Rollins favored him with an icy stare. "What did you think we were, a welcomin' committee? What's your handle—I mean, what you call yourself at the moment?" His voice was tinged with sarcasm.

"Laramie Nelson. I'm a Pinkerton, mister. My boss sent me into this jungle after a bandit gang that's been terrorizin' the stage lines."

Nobody seemed impressed. Morris said, in an attempt at humor, "And I'm the long-lost Queen of the May!"

"I'm a Pinkerton, Rollins, Laramie Nelson."

"You said that before. Go through him, Ince."

Ince made a good job of it. He lifted Laramie's sixgun, hunting knife and a roll of bills, but left his tobacco sack and cigarette papers.

As he patted Nelson over, none too gently, he felt a rustle of paper in a shirt pocket. He brought forth a worn square of paper, shook it out and regarded it closely.

"Find his Pinkerton credentials?" inquired Rollins, with a laugh.

Laramie gulped. He felt shaken, for in the press of things, he'd forgotten something.

"Nope. But look at this, Rollins!"

Rollins accepted the soiled sheet and read aloud: "Thousand Dollars Reward, Dead or Alive. Murder and Highway Robbery. Laramie Nelson, alias Colorado Red, alias Slim the Eel. Dangerous. Will Shoot to Kill. Notify Taylor, Sheriff, Provo, Utah Territory."

Rollins studied the photograph printed on the circular, and looked closely at Laramie. "It's him, no doubt about it."

"Look, Rollins, that circular is a plant! My boss had it printed in Fort Smith. He figgered if I bumped into any outlaws, they'd search me sure, and that would fool 'em. Peters kept my papers—"

"You talk too much," broke in Rollins. "But nice try, Laramie, Red or Eel. You shouldn't have been so proud of your dirty rep as to tote that circ on you. Last two cusses we snaffled claimed they were honest cowboys huntin' strays, only they had pokes and trinkets took from stage robberies in their saddlebags. Keep a close eye on him, gents. We'll add him to the gather and start home. Seven—and not one of us even wounded much. Reckon the Judge'll be pleased."

II

Laramie decided to accept the situation philosophically. There was nothing else he could do anyhow. He'd lost some time, true, but back in Fort Smith, he could soon prove his identity.

One deputy rode ahead, holding the lariat which was still around Nelson's neck; they'd hoisted the prisoner aboard Wingfoot.

He could hear the others talking behind him, and Rollins was saying, "Well, we didn't get any hint about that so-called Emperor or King of the Nations, but if there is such a man, I bet we caught a few of his boys. Ammo's runnin' low, and so's food, and we got to feed the prisoners."

"The Emperor or King of the Nations," thought Laramie. Brock might be right, when he said there was a rumor a particularly clever bandit chief had set himself up in the Indian Nations, and was directing operations. It had sounded ridiculous at first, but these officers seemed to believe it, that the most dangerous outlaws in the West had joined the "Emperor's" organization.

"I reckon we'll hunt a long while more 'fore we smell out Mazzotti's hideout," observed Ince.

So they had somehow learned the name, "Mazzotti."

"I still say we should've trailed them robbers a while longer," said Morris. "They might've led us to the place."

"How could we, when they spied Murph?"

"Okay," growled Murphy, "blame it all on me!"

"Your ears are too big," jested Morris. "They stick out past the chaparral."

Everybody chuckled and the tension eased. They pushed along a winding animal trail, finally coming to a wooded glade by a spring.

Curiously, Laramie took in the scene. Six men, each with leg irons on an ankle, were shackled to a chain with the cuffs spaced along it. They sat in a close circle, sullen expressions on their faces.

Two more deputy marshals, badges on, were guarding

the prisoners. One held a double-barreled shotgun and the other a 15-shot Henry rifle. Both wore Colts at their waists as well.

"You got another," said a thin man, dark circles under tired eyes.

"We got him, Yap," nodded Rollins. "You and Buff have any fuss with 'em while we were gone?"

"Nope, they're tamed, they don't like buckshot."

The riders dismounted. Ince and Murphy pulled Laramie off Wingfoot. He was shoved down and the last shackle in the chain was snapped on his ankle. An officer removed the handcuffs, and Laramie sat where he'd landed, looking at the other captives.

"Full house," said Rollins with satisfaction.

"You got nice equipment, Rollins," remarked Laramie.

A young fellow next to Laramie laughed at this, and others grinned. They thought the new prisoner was being sarcastic.

Rollins paid no attention. "Ince, you and Murph fetch up their horses. We'll hogtie 'em aboard and run 'em back to the wagon. Leave the ankle shackles on, so one don't get a notion of makin' a break for it. Wagon's four or five miles away."

Laramie took another look at his fellow prisoners. The one who'd laughed at what he considered Laramie's jest about the equipment was very young. Hardly twenty. He had innocent pale-blue eyes and the beard on his tanned face was more of a fuzz than whiskers.

"I'm called Babyface," the boy said. "Glad to meet you, mister. But you ain't one of our boys, are you?"

"No, but I was hopin' to be, till these hounds trapped me. I come from a long way off."

"Hey, Rollins," sang out a plug-ugly down the line. "We're hungry. How 'bout makin' a fire and heatin' some jerky and coffee, or do you aim at starvin' prisoners to death these days?"

"It would be better'n Judge Parker's drop, Benson. But we'll feed you. No fires, though. You can chew cold jerky and hardtack."

Benson cursed the marshal's heart and soul, but Rollins paid no heed. Ince and Murphy disappeared into the thick chaparral. Laramie could hear them moving around, and soon caught the beat of hoofs.

Babyface said cozily, "How many men you kilt, amigo?"

"Six to date," replied Laramie. "Maybe a few died after I took off. You can't blame me if they bled to death."

Babyface laughed over this. "You're a real card, friend. Well, I beat you by eight, and you're older'n I am."

Rollins had relit his cheroot and was squatting nearby; he overheard Babyface's boast. The chief of the marshals said coldly, "You forgot to mention those two little kids you drilled, son. Then there were the young girls you abused till they died from it."

Laramie realized he was chained next to a young monster, a child killer and a rapist. He took another unbelieving look at his new friend. Still, he couldn't see anything, except that Babyface's pink upper lip had a queer twist to it.

Nelson fitted right in with the circle of dirty, bearded men. He hadn't shaved for a week and had dressed to play the part of a bandit.

The horses were being lined up; they seemed uneasy, snorting and pulling back so that the officers had their hands full, trying to quiet them. And suddenly Benson

18

began cursing Rollins in a hoarse and loud voice, almost shouting.

"Shut up or I'll buffalo you!" snapped Rollins, starting at the troublemaker.

At that instant a deafening fusillade erupted. It tore leaves and branches from the nearby bushes, slugs whistling like droning bees all around. Laramie tried to jump up but Babyface knocked him flat. "Stay low! Stay low!"

The prisoners were all hugging the ground, keeping their heads down.

Laramie watched with incredulous eyes. Rollins had swung to shoot back into the chaparral, but he was knocked sprawling, sieved with heavy bullets. Ince and Murphy got off a couple of hasty ones before they, too, were ripped to pieces. The hail of death was chest and head high, the slugs passing over the captives, who lay still, pressed to the ground.

Marshals Buff and Yap, who had been off a bit, reached the edge of the small clearing, but then they, too, went down.

Stunned, Laramie Nelson waited. The blasting guns stopped as suddenly as they had began, and he could smell the acrid blue powder smoke as it drifted slowly toward the apparently peaceful sky of the Indian Nations.

"They're all done for," called Benson. "Hold it up."

"Okay, Benny," replied a gruff voice.

They sat up now, including Laramie. Toughs broke from the chaparral, smoking-hot repeating rifles in hand. "Hey Jed," sang out Benson. "Get the keys off Rollins and turn us loose, will you?"

The man called Jed was one of the most powerful looking fellows Laramie had ever seen. He stood over six feet, deep and wide of chest, muscled, hairy arms, and his strong legs were clad in leather. A wiry black beard stuck from his prognathous chin, and his mouth showed brutal determination. He ordered, "Check 'em all and put finishers into 'em."

He went to Rollins, crumpled on his face, gun by his outstretched hand. Jed kicked the lifeless body several times, cursing the dead deputy leader. He rolled Rollins over, found the shackle keys and tossed them to Benson. He stood up and fired three more unnecessary bullets into Rollins' head.

"That's from me, personal," he snarled, "for my dead brother you trapped and had dropped from Parker's hangin' machine."

Now he swept the pitiful remains of the dead officers, and remarked contemptuously, "Buzzard bait!"

Benson had freed himself and then passed the key along the line. The erstwhile prisoners, including Laramie, rose and stretched.

"Strip 'em, Benny," commanded Jed. He drew a Mexican cheroot from his pocket and lit it, blowing out a puff.

He watched Benson, who had evidently been leader of the party arrested by the deputies, as Benson and his friends went through the dead men's effects. "Take their badges," Jed said. "They may come in handy some time."

He signalled to Benson who went over to him. Laramie heard Jed say testily, "How in hell did you manage to get took, Benny? Another hour, we'd have been too late. Lucky one of the boys heard shootin' and hustled to fetch me. We aimed to meet you on your way back from that job across the river. When he swung over here, we spied

20

Rollins and some of his men in that valley and were able to get in close."

Babyface had heard this, too, and he called, "Jed, thank this hombre, Laramie, for that. They spent a lot of time trappin' him."

Jed frowned. He turned from Benson and came closer, staring at Laramie Nelson. "Who is he?" he asked Babyface.

"A good hombre, Jed, wanted for murder."

"Rollins has a circular on me in his shirt pocket," said Nelson.

"Go get it, Babyface," ordered Jed.

Babyface found the Wanted notice. There were bulletholes in it now but it was still readable. Jed scanned it and asked, "Utah. What you doin' way over this way, Laramie, or whatever you call yourself."

"A posse downed my whole band in a shootout near Durango in Colorado after a bank holdup. I had a hell of a time bustin' out of that ring. They chased me for a hundred miles and two good horses dropped dead under me 'fore I managed to shake 'em off."

Laramie could tell that Jed wasn't stupid, by any means, and he'd have to prove himself before the big fellow would accept him.

"You still ain't told me why you're this far east in the Territory."

"They had alarms out for me all through the west, and I come near gettin' trapped several times. I heard there was some mighty good hombres hidin' out in the Nations, so I headed this way."

Jed puffed on his cheroot for a time. Then he asked, "You any good with safes?"

"Sure. It's my specialty." As he said it, Nelson wondered if he'd have to prove it. He'd learned enough in his career to do so if necessary, but he hoped it wouldn't be.

"Bueno. The big ones 're too heavy to tote off and half the time it's too noisy blowin' 'em where they stand. Might be I can use you." He turned to his men. "Hustle, let's ride. Could be another bunch of Parker's marshals around and they'd have heard the gunfire."

The freed prisoners quickly armed themselves and found their mounts. Laramie retrieved his own weapons and claimed Wingfoot. "Fine animal," observed Jed. "Where'd you steal him?"

"Fancy horse breeder in Texas on my way over."

The dead were left for the vultures and coyotes, but the bandits took along their horses, guns and valuables. Benson brought a leather pouch to Jed and handed it over.

"You get the big one from Van Buren?" demanded Jed.

Benson seemed uneasy at this. "Nope, it didn't work out, Jed. Too many guards around. Got some cash and trinkets, though."

Jed grunted, frowned and took charge of the pouch. He said, "*He* ain't goin' to like it, Benny."

Benson gulped and looked even more worried.

They all mounted and Jed led the way, roughly southwest. As they came out on a higher crest, Laramie saw pine-covered mountains with bare red peaks thrusting to an azure sky. He soon realized that Jed had signalled that the recruit was to be watched.

Babyface rode by him, chatting gaily of murder and rape, hungrily asking details of Laramie's supposed crimes. This was easy, since Nelson simply described bloody events, putting himself in the place of outlaws he'd downed, making it sound like he was the lawbreaker instead of the lawman.

There wasn't the slightest chance of making a break for it now, even if Laramie had desired. Right behind rode a lean, sallow-faced bandit Babyface addressed as Lance. Lance had a thin, saturnine look, and would only grunt now and again; talking was evidently not his line. Twice, when Laramie let Wingfoot lag, Lance hit Wingfoot's rump with his quirt.

All around them was the vast maze of Indian Territory into which so many tribes had been driven by the conquering white men. Yet you could ride for miles and never sight a redskin.

The Arkansas River separated the Nations from Arkansas; several more rivers threaded the wilderness, the north fork of the Red, the Washita and Canadian, the Cimarron, while lakes and small tributaries abounded. Far to the south lay the Choctaw Plains, an expanse of blood-red prairie, which were fine grazing grounds. But here the jumbled hills and mountains dominated the land.

Laramie had a rough idea of where they were and the sun told him what direction they were traveling, otherwise he was lost in the jumble. They skirted high points, forded shallows, seeming to know where quicksands lay. Rabbits, birds and larger game fled before them.

He wished Brock Peters was riding by him. In the same fix.

He was not tied and he had his guns. But he was not free. One wrong play and they'd sieve him, even if he could take a couple along with him, and his name would be added to the heroic list of Pinkertons killed in line of duty!

III

The wanted circular and his being under arrest had helped him. So had his tough getup and histrionic abilities. Babyface taking a shine to him was good, too. It was just a hunch, but Nelson thought it was a tossup as to whether Jed would have killed him and dumped him. Wingfoot was a top animal, and Jed has cast several envious glances at Laramie's horse.

"Lucky you done fell in with us," Babyface was saying. "Otherwise you'd be bait for Judge Parker's hangin' machine." He lowered his voice. "Look, when you see the Chief, be mighty careful. His say-so means life or death, savvy?"

"I savvy, and gracias, Babyface. I kind of figured Jed was the man."

"Naw, he's one of the heads, but he ain't the top boss. Know what they call our chief? Emperor of the Nations, ain't that a good one? But he really is. Takes a strong hand to control a passel of men like us, yessir."

"Emperor of the Nations! Where is he?"

"At Headquarters. He don't ride out, just makes the plans. We got spies pass the word to us, mighty fine system. A small gang's got no chance against Parker's marshals, this way it's different. You seen that just now."

They rode down into another creek valley and Jed put his horse into the shallows along the bank but didn't cross the stream. He kept on west, the animals splashing along, so they left no trail that could be followed.

After a half mile, a red rock wall seemed to block the way entirely; cottonwoods and brush formed a dense screen. Jed swung sharply, and Laramie, coming along with the crew, saw a narrow opening through which the stream purled. There were bluffs on both sides, and they were challenged by riflemen posted above. Jed sang out, and they passed through.

To Laramie's astonished eyes, a wide, fertile valley stretched before them. Long ago, beavers had dammed the creek and there was a pond with a waterfall emptying from it.

Tepees, tents, log-and-brush shacks, were scattered out. There was one long building with mud walls and a roof of shakes, with a padlocked door, probably a storehouse. There were oasts, stone fireplaces for cooking and warmth.

Across the pond were several pole corrals, filled with mustangs and also some steers, no doubt for food purposes. Nelson sighted several goats cropping weeds and roots on the hillside.

On his right the ground rose gradually, with a winding path leading to the mouth of a large cavern halfway up the slope.

Men gathered about the incoming party, tough looking whites, dirty and bearded, wearing sixguns and sheathed hunting knives. There were also a scattering of Indians in Levi's and moccasins, coppery torsos bare, black hair banded with snakeskins. In the background Laramie saw squaws at work, and a couple of white girls, who looked bedraggled and abused, captive women.

Jed slipped from his sweated saddle and tossed his rein to a young squaw who had hurried to his side. "Break up, boys. Lance, you and Babyface watch out for Laramie." When he said "watch out," Laramie knew it meant the recruit was to be closely guarded.

Jed turned to Benson, and spoke, rather coldly to him. "Benny, stand by till I call you, savvy?"

25

Benson nodded and gulped. He sat down and fixed a quirly. Laramie noticed his hands were shaking as he lit up.

· "Come on, Laramie," said Babyface. "We'll cross over and turn our animals into the corrals.'

Most of the party had already crossed below the pond, and Nelson, trailed by Babyface and the dour Lance, went over, leading their mounts. He unsaddled Wingfoot, rubbed him down with the thick pad, and turned his pet mount into a big corral; there was hay and grain available, and a wooden chute carried water into a long trough so the critters could drink as they pleased.

They went back and settled down under a tall cottonwood. There was a small stone hearth with a blackened iron spit where they could cook. "This is our place," announced Babyface cheerfully. "Make yourself at home."

Laramie threw down his blanket roll and lounged by it. He looked around. Some of the bandits had squaws serving them. Bottles and steaks were appearing, biscuits being baked in Dutch ovens.

Laramie felt suddenly hungry.

Babyface drew a flask from his roll, took a swig and passed it to Laramie. The burning whiskey was a pickup that Nelson needed. He felt grateful as it warmed his insides.

He held the bottle out and Babyface offered it to Lance, who said sourly, "If somebody don't get busy around here, we'll starve." He went over and began to prepare a meal. They had a covered box dug into the ground in which they kept supplies.

Babyface laughed. "Don't pay no mind to Lance," he said loudly. "Inside he's as rotton as any of us!"

Lance didn't even glance around.

"The chief'll want to look you over, Laramie," said Babyface. "Nobody jines up till he says so. Jed'll show him that circular on you, don't worry."

The steak was beginning to sizzle as Lance fanned up the fire under the grill. A small pan of water was heating for coffee, and Lance found several sourdough biscuits, previously cooked, which he placed on the sides of the grill to warm them.

Before the meal was ready, Jed appeared outside the cave mouth, and sang out, "Come up here, Benny. Fetch along the new man."

Benson gulped. He dropped his gunbelt and hung it on a handy tree limb, then came over and said, "Shuck your gun and knife, you," he said sullenly. "Nobody who's armed goes near the chief, savvy? You better keep it in mind." He swung and started for the path up the hill.

Nothing to do but play along. Laramie gave his revolver and long knife to Babyface to keep for him. Benson was ahead, on the way to the high, wide entrance into the cavern.

The sun was low over the western mountains, rays slanting into the front of the big cave. As Laramie went in, he was surprised to see that the cavern opened out into a high-roofed chamber the size of a ballroom. Animal pelts were scattered about and the walls were hung with the stuffed heads of bison, deer and antelope.

It was cooler in there. A draft came through, and there was a strange, low moaning sound which increased and diminished. Laramie decided there must be a big crevice or opening of some sort which would run to the crest of the hill, but he couldn't see anything much in the darkening depths. He did hear the faint gurgle of water,

27

maybe a spring which ran down from the surface above.

Lanterns hung from spikes driven into the red rock walls. On the far side he saw a wide sleeping couch, more pelt rugs, clothing and assorted belongings on a rack. There were three large padlocked chests close to the head of the bed.

He jumped as a cold voice suddenly said, "H'm— h'm—well, Benson—h'm—what's the alibi—h'm—"

Laramie placed the speaker, who sat on a thronelike seat cushioned with furs, in a recess near the couch and chests.

His first impression was a massive head, completely bald, shining in the lanternlight. The intense blue eyes sunk deep on either side of a vulture beak fixed Benson, who stood before him, Jed off to one side.

Laramie could make out scarlet splotches on the man's head and pasty cheeks. He was sure no doctor, he couldn't diagnose skin diseases, though he'd seen smallpox sores and other blemishes. He wouldn't have recognized *lupus vulgaris,* red wolf, if he'd studied it in broad daylight, and maybe most physicians didn't know it or how deadly it was, except that sunlight would aggravate it and soon kill its victims.

He could only surmise the strange man was thin, for his body was swatched in a dark-silk robe; the clawlike hands sticking from the sleeves had the red blemishes on them, too.

Benson was rattled. He stammered, "Mr. Mazzotti, I done the best I could. Fetched back a thousand cash, 'sides watches and rings."

"H'm—h'm you were to bring me fifteen thousand dollars—h'm—the payroll being transported—h'm—to

28

Fort Smith. H'm—you failed."

"They had it locked in a safe weighed half a ton, bolted to the wagon bed. We downed the guards but couldn't budge the safe or open it. The shootin' fetched a passel of police on us. We just did manage to make it back across the river."

Jed listened, silently.

"H'm—you also walked into a trap—h'm—laid· by Judge Parker's marshals—h'm. If I hadn't sent Jed out to—h'm—watch for you and make sure you—h'm—got back, the others, my good men—h'm—would not be captives—h'm. Get out, Benson—h'm—Jed, the dam needs repairing. H'm—put this man on the job—get him—h'm—out of my sight!"

Mazzotti flushed so with rage that the rest of his complexion almost matched the scarlet blemishes.

Benson turned and slunk out. He glanced at Jed, appealingly, but the big fellow just shrugged and looked away.

Mazzotti produced a golden snuffbox, took a pinch in his long fingers, and delicately sniffed it up a nostril. He sneezed, then repeated the process in the other, wiping his face with a large silk kerchief.

He clapped his hands and a young woman emerged from the shadows. "A drink, my dear," he said. For the first time, his harsh voice softened.

She fetched a pitcher and poured a white liquid into a gold goblet encrusted with gems. "Jed," she said, "we need more goat's milk. Uncle Ferdinand has been drinking more lately."

She had a soft, pleasing voice, and Jed said, "Sure, Miss Nora, I'll see to it right off."

Now Jed shoved Laramie forward. "Here's the one, Wanted circ says he's a killer. And he claims to be a good safe man."

Mazzotti let him stand for a time. The deep-set eyes seemed to drill into Laramie, who shifted uncomfortably. The gaze was almost hypnotic. The angry flush on Mazzotti's face had faded, so the red blemishes stood out on the cheeks, the flesh reminding Laramie of a frog's belly.

Mazzotti drank slowly and handed the goblet back to Nora. Laramie had a good look at her. Long golden braids hung over her full bosoms, ribbon bows decorating the ends. She wore soft white buckskin and moccasins, a comfortable outfit. When she saw Laramie watching her, she smiled and nodded.

Finally Mazzotti spoke, his nervous speech habit breaking his voice. "H'm—h'm." He didn't sound too pleased. "Take him away, Jed—h'm. I'll think on it—h'm—meanwhile, watch him day and—h'm—night."

"Yessir." Jed took Laramie by the arm and started him toward the exit.

"Thank you, sir," called Laramie, but Mazzotti didn't glance at him again.

Nelson found he was sweating as they started down the path. He asked, "What you think, Jed? Will he take me in?"

"You better hope so. I told him you claim to be an expert safecracker and we need one. Parker's deputies trapped the best box-opener we had, in Van Buren a month ago."

"That's a mighty pretty wife he's got."

Jed snorted. "Wife, that ain't his wife! Chief don't trust females, 'cept Nora, she's his niece. Cooks his food and sees to him. Now go have a bite, Lance and Babyface'll show you the ropes. And don't wander around—savvy?"

Laramie savvied. He was on a shaky probation, teetering between thumbs up or thumbs down.

IV

Babyface and Lance were watching and he joined them. Jed went to a shack close to the storehouse. His squaw greeted him, and followed him inside. Babyface said, "Cook yourself a steak, Laramie, help yourself to coffee and biscuits. You stick with us."

"Suits me." Nelson went and threw a chunk of beef on the grill, hunkering there as it sizzled.

Other groups were scattered around the large encampment, eating and drinking. Some had squaws to serve them, and he noticed a couple of miserable looking white girls up the way. Indian women were bred to wait hand-and-foot on their mates, while the white females were unwilling captives.

Laramie was really hungry; when his steak was cooked, he took a couple of warm biscuits from the side of the grill and poured a tin mug of coffee, taking his heaped tin plate over and squatting by Babyface. They ate silently; then Babyface brought over cans of tomatoes and peaches, all the comforts of home.

The sun enlarged and reddened as it dropped to the western summits and shadows lengthened over the great arena. Laramie saw armed men converging and lining up at a point toward the entrance gap. He watched curiously as a tall, wide-shouldered man with erect military carriage appeared. He wore a faded gray uniform, a sash, and a saber was at his side as well as a large horse pistol.

"That's Colonel Riley," Babyface told him, as Laramie

stared at the proceedings. "He was colonel in the Confederate army when he was only twenty or so and he never forgot it."

Riley's snappy commands drifted to them on the breeze. Each man checked his rifle and Colt, and it reminded Laramie of an army change of guard as some of the force marched toward the east gap, while others picked up horses for mounted duty. Many older outlaws were veterans, Confederate or Union, and some had ridden for notorious guerrilla chiefs, such as Mosby and Quantrill.

He didn't see Jed. He asked Babyface, "Ain't Jed boss here, I mean outside of Mazzotti?"

"He's only one, he's a field general, sort of, Riley's in charge of security here. Another important cuss is Felipe Gomez, he handles raids to the southwest, and right now he's out with his crew on a job. We got informers, too, tip us off on big shipments."

Well, thought Laramie, it would take more than a handful of deputies to seize this stronghold. The U.S. Army would have a hard fight; they'd need artillery to smash through that east gap, and even then it wouldn't be too easy.

The night guard disappeared, and the day sentinels began drifting in.

Babyface prattled along about murder, rape and robbery, but Lance contributed only grunts or shrugs to the conversation as they smoked after the meal. Lance was taciturn, unfriendly.

As night fell, they shook out their blankets and lay down, hats for pillows. Babyface had thrown more wood on the fire, and its heat was welcome in the fast cooling mountain air. Laramie was happy to rest; he lay for a time, looking through the tree branches at the vast dome of the sky. Soon the moon came up, paling the myriad stars.

Babyface was on one side of him and Lance on the other; they had been delegated by Jed to keep an eye on the recruit.

He heard many low sounds from the camp. Horses snorted and stamped in the corrals across the creek; a cow would bawl or a goat bleated, and as the moon rose higher, coyotes began baying from hilltops, seeming to try and outdo one another in their strange songs.

"You asleep yet, Babyface?" he asked.

"Nope. What you want?"

"How's the pay in this outfit? Jed give what was fetched in to Mazzotti."

"You get plenty, cash, and Mazzotti pays fine if you can deliver. He likes gold and trinkets; keeps such stuff locked in them chests you must've noticed when Jed took you in. See, nobody jines up with us 'less Mazzotti says so."

Nelson saw two figures coming slowly down the path from the cavern in the moonlight, and propped up on an elbow to watch. One looked like Ferdinand Mazzotti, Emperor of the Nations, in his flowing robe. He thought the second was Nora, and the man held her arm as they strolled west along a beaten track.

Babyface noticed his interest and warned, "Lie quiet. He likes to walk in the moonlight, never comes out in the sun. Though when it's clouded up durin' the day, you might see him."

"That Nora's a beauty, ain't she?"

Babyface smacked his lips. "She sure is. Wish I had her alone, makes a man's mouth water, don't she? But if

33

Mazzotti ever catches you sheepeyein' her, he'll have Riley put you in front of a firin' squad, don't forget it. Not a man in camp wouldn't like to grab her, but nobody dares go near her. You better keep that in mind."

"I sure will."

"Shet up, the two of you, lemme sleep," growled Lance, rolling over. "You both make me sick."

Laramie lay back. Brock Peters had sent him deep into the Territory to find out what was going on, and Laramie sure had. It was a great deal more than he'd expected. He couldn't even figure how to extricate himself from this giant rattrap, let alone smash the powerful paramilitary organization built up by Ferdinand Mazzotti.

Finally he slept...

...Next thing he remembered, he was looking into the cherubic countenance of his Pinkerton superior, Brock Peters, and Peters was saying, "All you got to do is ride into the Nations and smell out that den of robbers. Maybe you can bust 'em up by yourself. If not, I know Judge Isaac Parker, and he'll give you a few of his deputy marshals to side you. Should be easy." And he heard himself saying, "I just resigned from the Pinkertons, Brock!"...

He jumped awake, sorry to find he'd only been dreaming. Ruby and purple streamers showed in the eastern sky, a magnificent spectacle heralding the rising sun. Only it didn't impress Laramie, he'd seen plenty of glorious dawns, and all he did was resume that gnawing worrying.

Lance was stirring around, shaking up the breakfast fire. Babyface grunted, stretched and cursed as he sat up. They fixed cigarettes and lit up.

34

Lance got the water boiling and threw in handfuls of coffee. He started strips of bacon frying in a greasy skillet, an appetizing odor wafting to Nelson's nostrils. There was a Dutch oven in which to bake sourdough biscuits, and Laramie went to give a hand. Other groups were coming to life, while squaws busily fixed breakfast for their masters.

Laramie yawned as he sat down with a tin plate heaped with bacon and warm biscuits. He had a tin cup of coffee strong enough to float a horseshoe. Babyface was busy stoking up, too. Lance crouched on his haunches, eating rapidly, washing down big mouthfuls with swallows of Arbuckle. He kept off a bit to himself; he seemed to be a lone wolf.

Nelson and Babyface finished eating and lit cigarettes. "Just where in hell are we?" asked Laramie. "Somewheres in the Nations, I savvy that. I been to Fort Sill, but that's west of here, and I ain't really been all through Indian Territory."

"I have, I was brought up around here. Way south is the blood-red mud of the Choctaw Plains, then the Chickasaws, Creeks and Seminoles, and Cherokees, they were called the 'Five Civilized Tribes or Nations.' They're in the eastern part of I.T. So then the U.S. Govament starts pushin' one tribe after another in as they were conquered. Southwest are some Arikarees, and over Fort Sill way they got all the Kiowas and Comanches they can round up off the Texas Panhandle. They shoved Osages in next the Cherokees, who are up north—this here is the south rim of the Osage Nation, see? Cherokees and Osages fight among themselves some, but they settle things in their own Indian courts."

35

"Huh. How come the Osage let a bunch of white men take over like they have here?"

Babyface grinned. "Osages think this place is ha'nted, see? We got a couple breed renegades wanted by their people for murderin' their own tribesmen. An Indian court would condemn 'em to death, so they tell us. Osages call that cavern Cave of the Spirits. They say their ancestors walk around here nights, moanin' and groanin'."

Laramie recalled the soughing wind sounds he'd heard in Mazzotti's lair.

"Yessir, we're safe here," went on Babyface. "That east gate is guarded day and night, and we keep patrols around the valley. This crik runs into the Kiamichi River."

Laramie had made a careful study of the map of Indian Territory which Brock Peters had shown him. He had a keen memory and good sense of direction, and with what Babyface had just told him, he had a better idea of where the fortress was located.

He roughly estimated the mileage from the time it had taken him to ride from the Arkansas after crossing near Fort Smith, then the distance from where he'd been first captured by the deputy marshals and then snatched away by Jed's party.

"I'd just like to see a passel of Parker's deputies try to bust in here," gloated Babyface. "They'd be wiped out. Only a trained Injun scout could even sneak up on us, and why should they bother? Osage are scared of the place."

Without realizing it, the talkative Babyface had given Laramie a hazy idea. Yes, Indians could do it—if they had a good reason. But the Osage evidently shunned the valley, and most Indians avoided attacking whites, that lesson had been brutally burned into their souls.

Jed emerged from his shack, smoking a twisted black cheroot. He glanced at the trio lounging near their cookfire. Laramie and Babyface waved a good morning but Jed didn't bother to wave back; he strolled on, and crossed the creek on a log and plank bridge.

Idly, Nelson kept turning over his idea in his mind. Indians could get in, at night. White riders in daylight would be shot down without a chance to put up a fight.

The sun came up and full daylight bathed the wilderness. A tall fellow with bony, wide shoulders and a narrow waist, a prizefighter's build, strolled over to the three as they lounged near their hearth. "Howdy, Huck" said Babyface, and Huck gave him a nod.

Now Huck faced Laramie, who was sitting with his back to the cottonwood. Nelson noticed one of Huck's eyes was mirled with marble-blue streaks; he had a broken snout and a long, badly healed knife scar down his brown cheek.

He spoke to Laramie. "I like your horse, mister. Give you fifty for him." It sounded like a command rather than an offer.

Laramie rose up. Tall as he was, Huck topped him by a couple of inches, and he was heavier, too. Nelson gave a fleeting smile. "Sorry," he drawled. "He ain't for sale."

Huck scowled. "I didn't ask you was he for sale, I said I'll give you fifty for him. You stole him somewheres anyhow. Here's your money." He tossed a roll of bills at Laramie, who kicked it back at him.

Nelson hadn't strapped on his gunbelt, but as far as he could make out, Huck wasn't armed, either.

Huck hit him without warning, a hard punch that rocked Laramie back on his heels; he followed up with a jolting left to the chin, but now Laramie was ready and sidestepped so the second blow lost most of its force.

V

From the way Huck handled himself, his footwork and the speed with which he struck, Laramie knew he was a trained fighter.

Huck had expected to land his second blow as easily as he had the first; before he could get on balance, Laramie clipped him alongside the head. Huck shook his head against the ringing in his ears. Nelson feinted, Huck thought he had an opening and bored in, but missed his strike, and this time Laramie got him with a right-left to the point of his jaw.

Nelson had been in plenty of rough-and-tumble scraps. He could quickly size up an opponent and figure weaknesses. He brought the back of his fist across Huck's eyes; Huck blinked away water blinding him for a moment, and as he pulled himself together, Laramie whipped him around with a stab to the nose and knocked Huck down with a vicious uppercut.

Laramie stepped back, waiting for him to get up.

"Shucks," said Huck. He spat blood, cursed, waggled a loose tooth, and pushing to his feet, walked off without another word.

"Nice goin', Laramie," said Babyface admiringly. "That Huck's a tough scrapper. Used to be a pro."

"He's got a glass jaw," shrugged Nelson, though he was somewhat surprised. Huck's heart hadn't really seemed to be in his work.

He looked around and watched as Huck went to his own camp and sat down, rolling a quirly. Then Laramie noticed Jed, cheroot in his teeth, standing nearby. Jed had watched the set-to. He felt a twinge of suspicion; Jed had made no attempt to interfere.

He decided to go over and wash his bruised jaw in the cool creek water, and then see how Wingfoot was getting along. He lay flat on the bank and rinsed his face and hands, wiping dry with his bandanna. Then he crossed the bridge and went to the corral where his pet horse stood. Wingfoot came to nuzzle his hand; he seemed to be fine, rested, well-fed.

A party of riders gathered down the line and headed west; probably a scouting or raiding band, he guessed.

Camp life bustled about him. Squaws were washing clothing on the creek banks, skirts hiked up, pounding men's dirty pants and shirts with stones to get them clean. Card games went on here and there. A man with a guitar, wearing a sombrero and Mexican garments, strummed on a guitar, while another played a mouth organ.

Nelson started to stroll back to his spot and was almost there when somebody spoke up behind him. He turned, confronting a fellow with the build of a champion wrestler. The man was a hulking giant, and lumbered up. His clothing was filthy, and he hadn't shaved or washed for a month, decided Laramie. He could smell the body odor a yard away.

"What's the idea, boy, pickin' on my pard Huck that way?" he demanded.

Here we go again, thought Laramie.

And as he glanced around, sure enough, Jed was watching, hands clasped behind his back, the smoking cheroot stub in his teeth.

For an expert infighter like Laramie Nelson, the chief problem in tangling with such an opponent as this was to prevent him from getting a bear grip, for he could crush a man's ribs with those terrible arms, held out at his sides like a gorilla.

Actually, despite his size and weight, he was easier than Huck had been, for he was ponderously slow and telegraphed all his punches.

The lithe Laramie danced around, tapping him, stinging him to irritate him so he'd lose all caution. The giant swore at him, and began puffing; he didn't like prancing at all.

When he had the big fellow just where he wanted him, Laramie jumped in and drove his hard fist with all his weight behind it into the softened, fat belly.

The ape doubled up. Laramie chuckled and caught him under the chin with his knee, nearly cracking the jaw. The big man sat down hard, a dazed look in his piggy eyes.

It took him quite a while to regain his wind. He slowly pushed himself up, bottom first, like a cow pushing itself out of a bog, shaking his head.

Suddenly his face broke into a hideous grin, showing stained teeth, two front ones missing.

"Boy—you're awright. I'll—put my money on you—for champ—any day!" Not at all annoyed, he waved to Laramie and waddled off.

Laramie's jaw ached from the surprise punch Huck had landed, and his knuckles were raw. He went back, strapped on his gunbelt, set his Stetson on his head and started slowly off. Some of the bandits who'd seen the two scraps waved and grinned at him. Babyface and Lance didn't trail him but were watching.

He didn't see Jed, but as he came to a spot where he could see around the near end of the long storehouse, he spied Jed unlocking the padlock on the door. He hurried over.

"Jed!" he sang out.

Mazzotti's big field general turned to face him. He wore a walnut-stocked .45-caliber Frontier Model Colt in an open holster, rawhide string at the bottom tied to his leg to keep it from flapping.

"What now?" asked Jed.

Laramie kept back a few paces. "Call off your dogs, Jed," said Nelson coldly. "Or—" He broke off, holding Jed's hard stare without flinching.

"Or what?" growled Jed.

"Or you can take ten paces, count to three, draw your hogleg and we'll settle in here and now. Your boys'll kill me, but you go to hell along with me."

Suddenly Jed laughed. "Aw right, Laramie. No hard feelin's. Just testin' you out, had orders to, savvy? 'Fore long, we'll see if you're as good at openin' safes as you are at fighting."

Jed turned and opened the storehouse door, went inside. Laramie glimpsed piles of cases, rifles and ammunition, blasting powder and caps, canned goods, bags of coffee and grain, bales, everything such a camp might require.

Actually, Laramie was greatly relieved. He'd felt he had to call Jed's bluff—if it had been a bluff. It had been a dangerous gamble; if he'd lost it, he'd have been slaughtered. But evidently he'd made the right play. He'd shown he could fight and wasn't a man to be bullied.

Lance and Babyface were waiting for him. Babyface had a pleased smile on his young face, as though aware of what had been going on.

It had taken nerve to brace Jed that way. Laramie felt sweat on his bronzed brow; he pushed back his hat and wiped his face. And again, as in his dream, he recalled how easy Brock Peters had said it would be to track down and defeat the gang operating from the Nations.

Suddenly he saw Nora coming down the path from the caverns. She was alone and the morning sun touched her golden hair; high in the azure sky, puffs of white cirrus clouds scudded along. Laramie hurried over toward the girl as she started west on the path.

"Hey, you, come back!" That was Lance, who jumped up, but Babyface held him back.

"Morning, Nora," called Laramie, and as she turned and smiled, he touched his hat brim and added, "Beautiful day, ain't it?"

"Oh yes, I do love such a morning!" She smiled brightly up at him. She was a ripe beauty, in her late teens, and Laramie could guess why she welcomed him. She was of an age when a girl thirsted for admiration and attention of males. The camp was filled with men who would gladly have competed for her favors, but none dared approach her because of her uncle's stern ban. "I'm going for a walk, won't you come with me?" She almost begged him to stay with her.

"It'll be a real pleasure." He was aware that many eyes watched as he strolled with Nora. Lance and Babyface trailed behind, but kept their distance; they'd been ordered to keep Laramie in sight.

Her shapely body was enticing in the soft doeskin. "I been wonderin' why a pretty girl like you would stick way out here in the monte," he said. "Fact, you're the most beautiful thing I ever did see!"

Flattery might get you nowhere sometimes, but Laramie had long ago found it never did any harm with a woman. Her full lips parted in a smile. "You don't really mean that, do you, Laramie?"

42

"I sure do, I move around a lot, and I've seen plenty of pretty girls from Mexico to California, but you beat 'em all."

That didn't hurt his stock, either. She sighed, deeply. "I have to stay here and take care of my uncle. When I was ten, Indians killed my parents, and Uncle Ferd adopted me like his own. He's been mighty good to me." She looked earnestly at him. "I noticed you when Jed fetched you into the front cavern."

Laramie was causing a sensation; somebody had called Jed, and the big fellow had come from the storehouse and stood, watching as Nora took Laramie's arm and they moved along like a pair of lovers.

"When I was in that cave," he said, "I felt a strong draft blowin' through. Must be an opening back there."

"Yes, there is. Several smaller caves are behind the main ones. I sleep there, and a slide slants up, all the way to the top of the cliffs. Uncle Ferd says the brook must've cut it; the water comes down that way."

"That's interesting. Is that slide hard to climb?"

"No, I've been up several times. It's easy if you keep low."

"I sure wish we could be alone together," he sighed, with a smitten look, and she flushed. "Whole camp's watchin' us."

After a moment, she said, "My uncle says I mustn't trust men."

"And he's right, usually, that is. You can only trust a few, say like me. I wouldn't harm you for all the gold in Californy, nossir. But—well, you draw me like a magnet draws a helpless piece of steel, Nora." He kept his voice respectful.

She was starved for such palaver. She thought for a

time, then said, "I can't come out through the front way, I'd be seen. But—well, my uncle sleeps in that side alcove with a screen around his bed. He sleeps so sound, I can't even wake him sometimes till late next day. He smokes a funny looking pipe, and takes medicine before he goes to bed."

"Is the pipe a long, straight bamboo stick with a little cup near one end?"

"Yes, how did you know, did you see it?"

"No, but I've seen others like that, out west mostly." He didn't tell her he'd been in Chinese opium dens, searching for robbers. "What if I could snake up and get back to where you are nights, Nora? We could climb that slide and walk in the moonlight, be alone a while."

He'd hit it right again. Plenty of girls liked to see their sweethearts secretly. "I'd like that," she admitted shyly. "But you wait till most everybody's asleep, mind you. There are night sentries but none stays close to the cavern. A rider patrols the north crest, but there's plenty of trees and bushes where it's easy to hide."

He knew the right mixture of boldness and considera- tion that would please a young female. "Tonight?" he said huskily. "Please! Maybe around one? The moon'll be up."

After a pause she agreed. "Tonight, then, unless I signal you. If it doesn't look just right, I'll show myself just before dark. But make sure nobody sees you come up the path, and when you get into the cavern, keep close to the far wall."

"You won't tell your uncle?"

"Oh, no. I'll mix him a real strong potion."

"I'll be there if I have to die for it!"

"I couldn't bear to have anything happen to you on my account, Laramie." She suddenly squeezed his hand. "We better get back. I have to fix my uncle's breakfast."

She turned and they hurried back, Lance and Babyface hastily retreating before them. Nora gave Laramie a fleeting smile and went nimbly up the path into the cavern. He watched her until she was out of sight, and then started to rejoin his two comrades who had gone back and sat by the dying cookfire.

But Jed stepped out, blocking his way. "Okay Laramie, you've done more'n enough to prove you got the nerve of a brass monkey. But don't go further, savvy? Keep away from that girl. I don't give a whoop in hell, but the Chief'll have Colonel Riley stand you in front of a firin' squad. I won't mention this to Mazzotti; I'll cover you if anybody else does, say you weren't warned, but now you know."

"Sure, sure. Listen, sittin' around gabbing don't intrigue me. When do we get a little action?"

"Keep your pants on. Spy come in at dawn with a message. Big job."

"Who's going?"

"Not many, it's job needs doin' on the q.t., and a big party would probably be spotted by Parker's marshals. They're on the prod since we wiped out Rollin's posse."

"Is it a safe?"

"Don't ask questions. Steer clear of Nora and of trouble. Lie low, get plenty of rest. When we get the word, we'll have to move fast. It'll be a few days 'fore the shipment gets to Fort Smith."

Jed swung away. Laramie shoved back his hat, made a cigarette, and returned to his roll. Lance snarled, "You jackass! Told you to stay away from that female! You're askin' for a slug in the guts."

"We warned you," nodded Babyface.

"I done forgot," said Laramie carelessly, blowing out a puff of smoke. He sat down, leaning against the big cottonwood.

"What'd Jed say?" asked Babyface curiously.

"Said he'd let it go this time but never try it again."

Lance swore in disgust and lapsed into his usual sullen mood. Babyface sighed. "Wisht I could get holt of her." The young killer was slavering, and his talk of what he'd do to Nora disgusted Laramie, but he said nothing. In due time, Babyface would answer for his crimes.

They ate at noon. It was heating up, and they stayed in the shade. Most men not on duty settled down for a siesta. Laramie slept as long as possible; he'd be busy that night and would need his rest.

The three roused after napping through the worst of the heat. The sun was halfway down to the western mountains. Others were coming alive. Guns began banging across the pond. "Target practice," said Babyface. "Let's go make some tin cans jump, then come back and play acey-deucy."

They crossed the bridge. In a corral, a couple of breeds were working with recalcitrant mustangs; goats climbed among the high rocks, nibbling leaves and roots. Below the dam, Laramie saw Benson, naked to the waist, and mud-splashed, slaving away with several other men.

Squaws and the captive women were fixing food, baking bread, washing and mending clothing—endless work for females. Squaws expected it, for Indian braves were hunters and warriors. Their women skinned and cut up the game killed, dried some, pounded nuts, berries and fat into the nourishing pemmican.

Both Lance and Babyface were good shots with pistol and carbine. The three wagered on how many hits could

46

be made when a can was tossed into the air. Laramie won two out of three, but Lance was almost as expert, and Laramie was just as glad not to look too fancy.

When they tired of this sport, they repaired to their camp and got out a greasy deck of cards. After a few hands, Laramie kept the stakes low; it was obvious the pasteboards were marked, so Laramie lost, gracefully.

After supper, Jed came along carrying a leather bag. He counted out money to each, then went on to another group. Lance grumbled, "Shucks, Laramie didn't even earn his pay last job."

"If it hadn't been for him comin' along and delayin' those marshals, we'd be rottin' in Parker's Hell on the Border!" said Babyface.

Laramie added the cash to a store he carried in a moneybelt next his hide. He had more stowed in his gear, distributed so it couldn't all be stolen at once. They fried steaks, had biscuits, canned tomatoes and peaches, plenty of strong coffee for supper.

The pot was left on the grid; the frying pan and greasy metal plates were carelessly wiped after being dipped in a bucket of water. Other groups stoked up; Jed and those with women to serve them ate in their tepees or shacks.

They smoked and lounged around. When dark fell, Laramie pulled up his blanket and lay down; he'd edged as far as he dared from his two custodians. He was glad to see Lance bring out a bottle, take a pull on it, and pass it to Babyface. If they downed enough rotgut whiskey, they'd sleep more soundly.

He dozed, aware of the many camp noises. Across the creek, the animals sounded off from time to time, and as the moon rose, coyotes began baying. Save for an occasional small cloud puff, the night was clear. The perimeter of camp was carefully patrolled by Riley's sentries, but the main section was considered safe.

Laramie Nelson was a trained scout; he'd had plenty of such experiences, for it was part of his business. He could move with animal stealth, like Indians on the prowl. Lance was a champion snorer; Babyface was young and slept soundly, and by ten o'clock, everybody had settled down.

After midnight, Laramie made careful preparations. He slipped from under his blanket, leaving his Stetson showing, stuffing boots and other gear under his covering so it looked like a sleeping figure. He left his cartridge belt and thrust his Colt and knife into his pants' belt. Moccasins on his feet, he began inching off. Trees here and there offered shadows away from the moon, and after a painfully careful progress, he made it up to the dark cavern mouth, snaking most of the way, knowing if he was caught, he'd be executed immediately.

VI

It was a relief to crawl in, lie flat and let his eyes adjust to the interior gloom.

As Nora had advised, he kept to the rock wall, well away from Mazzotti's alcove; the screens were up, and he listened for a time, making sure the strange Emperor of the Nations wasn't stirring in his niche behind the curtain.

A faint, acrid odor hung in recesses; he recognized the smell of burnt opium. Probably the sleeping potion Mazzotti took was a mixture of the drug, too. From time to time, the wind moaned in the rock chimney in the rear.

He rose and glided soundlessly over the packed shale flooring of the huge front cavern. He kept feeling the wall, turning with it; then he sighted a little beam of unsteady light, probably a candle lit by Nora in her alcove.

She was waiting for him; he saw her standing there, and went to her. She touched his lips with her fingers, cautioning silence. Blowing out the guttering candle, she took his hand to guide him into the depths.

The sound in the rill grew louder. Ahead of him, she kept hold of his hand, and soon they began to climb. It was steep, but they could make it, keeping down low, and before long, Laramie saw a faint shaft of moonlight.

Then they were up on the north rim of the valley. Rocks, trees and chaparral masked the opening where the tiny brook plunged into the bowels of the earth a few steps from where they stood.

"I'm mighty glad you let me come—" he began, but she touched his lips again.

He heard slow hoofbeats, and soon a horseman rode by, skirting the bower, moving westward along a beaten trail.

Coyotes were at it on distant hilltops; an owl hooted, the breeze rustled dry seedpods. Finally she spoke: "We can talk now. He won't be back for an hour. He'll ride all the way to the other end 'fore he turns."

"Nora," he whispered, "all I can think about is you."

"There's a place we can sit a while, but I don't dare stay long."

She led him to a flat stone; the rill ran before them, and they sat close together. Nelson put an arm around the girl's waist; sighing, she snuggled against him, and he was stirred by her. She was hungry for such attention, her whole nature cried for it, driving her to the man.

After a time he kissed her and she responded gladly.

"You shouldn't be way out in the wilds like this," he told her. "A woman needs a home and folks around,

49

decent folks. I could take you away from this place."

They talked, the girl close to him. He learned something about her. Her father had been Mazzotti's younger brother, and had come out to west Texas with his wife and child, Nora. They'd met her uncle in El Paso, where he'd owned an elegant hacienda; he'd been in Mexico and was very rich, she didn't know how he'd made his fortune. He was unmarried, and hadn't seen his only close relative, Nora's father, for over ten years. Her parents wanted to go to Arizona, which was just opening to settlement, despite the Apaches.

Ferdinand Mazzotti had been something of a recluse; a fat Mexican woman, Maria, had seen to the house and cooking. A small cavalry unit was heading west to garrison one of the forts erected to guard the route to California from the Indians, and Nora's parents decided to go with it, as did several other settlers.

Nora had been put in a convent school, her uncle paying all expenses, and then buying her father a covered wagon and equipment. He'd promised to care for the little girl till her parents were settled, when they would come for her.

"I'll never forget the day my uncle came to the school and told me the train had been ambushed in the *Canon de Muerte* by Apaches. My father and mother and everybody else in the party died there."

Soon, she'd gone to live with her uncle. Maria had been motherly and gladly saw to Nora's care. When the elderly woman had died, Nora was fifteen and had assumed the household duties . . . One night a mysterious courier had visited Uncle Ferd, who'd awakened Nora, told her they must leave immediately.

Mazzotti seemed to have plenty of money; with a few

packs and horses, they'd hurried into the wilds, crossing the dangerous trans-Pecos region, pausing now and then to rest. They hadn't stopped until they reached Indian Territory. Nora didn't know much about her uncle's business, but he knew how to contact such men as Jed and Riley, and had a genius for organization...

Laramie could more or less fill in the gaps. During the Mexican revolution, when Juarez and his *peones* had driven out the French and executed Maximilian, fortunes had been made smuggling arms and ammunition. Probably Mazzotti had acquired his in such fashion. Finally, some old enemy or the law had discovered him outside El Paso and he'd been warned in the nick of time, taken off...

She let Laramie kiss her and clung to him, soft arms around his neck. Finally she said, "We better get back. We can meet again soon—if you want."

"I sure do, Nora."

Her story had stirred him; he'd heard stranger tales during his travels, but he was sorry for Nora. She seemed inherently decent, and should have a chance to lead an honest life.

The patrolling sentry came back on the ridge, went on. Then the two made a cautious return down the slide, and Nora went to her bed. Laramie managed to reach his blanket without stirring any alarm. Lance was snoring, Babyface sound asleep.

He lay awake awhile, figuring it out. He had to get back to Fort Smith and talk with Judge Parker and his chief marshal, but plenty of help would be required.

He recalled this was Osage land; Indians could do the job better. The trouble was, they shunned the haunted caverns.

He finally slept, waking after dawn with the stirring camp. He had breakfast, washed up, smoked.

Camp life went on. Colonel Riley of the ramrod spine would review his changing of the guard, make his rounds.

Late in the morning, Laramie said, "How about a ride down the line, boys? My horse needs to stretch."

"Sure, we'll go with you," agreed Babyface.

The trio crossed to the corrals and saddled up. Wingfoot was glad to be on the move again, and stepped briskly out as they rode west through the valley, following the creek's course.

Babyface stayed alongside Laramie, talking away as usual; Lance stayed just behind. There was little or no chance to escape, for Laramie knew Lance would gladly shoot him if he tried to gallop away and shake the two detailed to watch him. And if he did get clear, it would alert the outlaws.

Twice they were hailed by sentries covering the trail, but the main encampment was at the eastern end of the valley, near the gap. After an hour or so, they returned to camp, Wingfoot exercized and Nelson thoughtful.

Several days passed.

It was monotonous, three meals a day, card games, target practice, talking, talking, talking. Laramie knew that by this time, Brock Peters must have chalked him up as the fifth Pinkerton who had died on this assignment.

He visited Nora on two nights, but during his return from the last rendezvous with the girl, he'd nearly been caught.

Nelson hated to lose Wingfoot but he could never escape on his own horse. Desperate, he thought of trying to seize the sentry on the north ridge some night, and taking his mount, for he had to have a horse to get away. But this would alarm the outlaws, even if he succeeded. He wasn't sure of the shortest route back to Fort Smith, and they might overtake him, shoot him out of the saddle.

He'd just about decided he'd have to chance this scheme, when Jed called him one bright morning.

"Awright, Laramie, come along." His tone was businesslike; Laramie started to strap on his gunbelt, but Jed ordered, "Leave that and foller me."

Jed took him up to the main front cavern.

Ferdinand Mazzotti was awaiting them, sitting on his throne-like chair.

Mazzotti began to speak as soon as Laramie stood before him. "I have just had word a good deal of money and gems will be held for a time in a safe in Fort Smith. The building is close to police headquarters, so it would be too noisy to blow the safe. This is a job for a small party, with an expert who can open the safe, for it is too heavy to be moved. Can you open it if taken to the spot?"

Laramie had arrested plenty of safecrackers, or boxmen as they were known in the trade. So he knew a good deal about the ticklish business. A top safecracker was among the elite of the criminal world.

"What make is the safe, sir?" he asked. "What model, what year was it manufactured?"

Mazzotti glanced at Jed, who shrugged. Nelson said, "It's like this, Mr. Mazzotti. I savvy how most safes are made; every one is a little different, but they fall into classes accordin' to how the tumblers operate."

"Can you or can you not open it?" Mazzotti spoke impatiently. The pupils of his eyes were like pinpoints— due to the opium he smoked, Laramie knew.

"Maybe, maybe not. There's some new ones out that you have to have the combo or else drill in and use explosives."

"I told you that's too noisy, to blow it!" Mazzotti was frowning. He was angry, with Jed rather than with Laramie. "After this, Jed," he said severely, "you will be able to supply such details."

He thought for a time, and finally said, "There's only one thing to be done. Go in and perhaps this man can handle the job. If not, they'll have warning, and we lose a small fortune. This time, so you will remember your lesson, Jed, you will lead the party. A large crew can't be taken along, it's too dangerous, for Parker's marshals are furious after what happened to Rollins and his posse."

"Yessir," said Jed. He added, sullenly, "If Judge Parker ever gets me before him in his court, I'm a dead man for sure."

Mazzotti shrugged coldly, and turned away. The interview was over.

Jed swung, and Laramie trailed him down the path. "When do we ride, Jed?" asked Nelson.

"When I tell you," snapped Jed, turning toward his shack. He was angry at having been called down before the recruit, and also at being ordered across the Arkansas into Fort Smith. Usually, as Laramie had gathered, Jed would escort raiders to within striking distance and wait to make sure they returned safely, as he had with Benson's bunch.

Laramie rejoined his two companions. "What was that all about?" asked Babyface.

"A job for me. I don't know when, though."

Time dragged. It usually grew very hot during the middle of the day but cooled off as the sun set. Twice there were fierce rainstorms with winds of almost tornado velocity, but the camp was well-protected and little damage was done.

Target shooting, card games, riding down the valley, always escorted by Lance and Babyface, Laramie thought the word would never come. When he tried to figure out some definite plan, when he did get out of the trap, he found it impossible. He'd have to play it as it developed.

At last, as Laramie roused from a siesta one afternoon, Jed came over to him. "Eat early, Laramie. Check your guns, and have your horse saddled and be ready to move out in about an hour. You, too, Lance, you're comin' with me."

"How about me?" asked Babyface.

Jed shook his head. "You stick to camp, boy."

He swung away and Laramie saw him speaking with Huck, the prizefighter with whom Laramie had had the little scrap.

VII

Jed took Laramie, Lance and Huck through the east gate. The tall, wide-shouldered Huck seemed to hold no hard feelings against Laramie because he'd been licked in the fist fight.

Wingfoot moved under him, with his tremendous, spirited power, that was a comfort. Jed was grumpy and had little to say, besides snapping an order now and again.

As they rode, Laramie took careful note of all landmarks, figured compass points by the sun; he thought he could find the valley again, in daytime, anyhow.

Each man in the small group had iron rations in his saddlebags, jerky, hardtack, deerskin pouches of pemmican supplied by squaws, which would supply plenty of energy on a long run, and could be eaten as a man rode along.

Dark fell, but Jed kept going, though he slowed the pace. He knew the trails and never hesitated. Laramie could check direction by the stars; then the moon came up, and they pushed along.

It was well after midnight before Jed called a halt, to blow the horses, unsaddle and rest. They camped on the bank of a small river, rubbed down the animals and drove the stakepins so the critters could water and graze. Jed wouldn't allow a fire, so they ate cold jerky, hardtack, washed down with water. They rolled in their blankets, head on saddle, and slept a few hours.

They were moving again at dawn, pausing only to blow the horses. Laramie felt better, with Wingfoot under him. He was at least free of the deadly valley trap, he had his carbine and Colt, and enjoyed the sensations of a man just released from prison.

In the afternoon, Jed slowed the pace, and Laramie heard him say to Huck, "Don't want to hit the river 'fore dark."

They were, Laramie knew, in the south Cookson Hills, beautiful country, with forest-clad peaks, and many blue lakes. North lay Tahlequah, capital of the Cherokee Nation; behind them, the Osage Nation had been squeezed in among the original Five Civilized Tribes.

Jed halted them in the afternoon, in dense woods through which coursed a small tributary of the Arkansas. They unsaddled, rubbed down the horses, and ate a bite. They could smoke, but no cookfire was built.

As night fell, from the height they saw lights of a town coming on. "There she is, Jed," said Huck. "Fort Smith."

Huck seemed to be a top man with Jed, a trusted member of the outlaw organization.

They saddled up again at dusk, and Jed led the way slowly through narrow trails; the glow of Fort Smith grew brighter, and finally they glimpsed the glint of lights on a broad river, the Arkansas.

Around midnight, Jed ordered, "Wait here, boys. Huck, you're in charge. You can smoke, but cup the matches when you light up."

He disappeared toward the river. When he returned, he said, "Foller me." They rode slowly for a short time until Jed said, "Get down, boys, lead your horses. It ain't far."

They pulled up in a grove; Laramie could see the Arkansas through the trees.

"Lance, you stick here with the horses. Huck, you and Laramie come with me."

Nelson started to pull his carbine from the boot, but Jed said, "Leave that, and your cartridge belt. We travel light from here on. Keep your sixgun and knife, put a few spare shells in your pockets. Shuck your boots and wear moccasins."

In Indian file they marched to the bank of the river, sheening in the moonlight; Fort Smith showed across the stream.

A skiff was drawn up in the sand and a dark figure stepped from the bushes, "Take us across, Eagleclaw," commanded Jed.

Eagleclaw was an Indian; his dark hair was banded with a snakeskin, his torso naked. He wore Levi's but his feet were bare.

They piled into the skiff. Eagleclaw rowed them swiftly across the river with long, powerful strokes of the oars.

They grounded in sand on the east shore, and left the dinghy. "Wait right here for us, Eagleclaw," said Jed. "Keep outa sight."

A buggy was tied to a tree limb near at hand. The three piled in, Jed handling the reins. They clopped to a lane, then onto a wider street, north toward the settlement's heart.

Jed pulled up in the shadows not far from a large brick structure. A lamp burned inside, and they glimpsed a man in uniform, a shotgun in his hands, pacing up and down in front on patrol.

"Go lay him out, Huck," said Jed. "Don't make any noise. Gag him, tie him good, and hide him. Then hustle on back here. We'll be waitin'. Take this rawhide and tie him tight but first make sure he don't yelp and give any alarm."

Huck jumped down from the buggy. They watched him as he made a stealthy approach. "Couple more inside," remarked Jed, after Huck had left them. "But I got a key to a back door. We'll put a gun on 'em and truss 'em up. Safe's in the central office."

Evidently, thought Laramie, the outlaw gang's spies sent detailed information to Mazzotti.

The uniformed guard came slowly around on his patrol and reached the south corner of the brick building. Just as he swung, a shadowy figure jumped out, grabbed him from behind, cutting off his wind, ramming a knee into the small of the victim's back.

Jed gave a satisfied grunt. "Huck's a good man. Time to go now, Laramie."

Laramie got out on his side. Jed went to secure the horse's rein to a post, and as he was busy at this, his back to Laramie, Nelson hit him an expert blow alongside the head with the barrel of his revolver. The crack of metal on bone sounded loud; Laramie hit Jed a second blow to be sure, and the big man's knees caved in.

Laramie dragged him around the far side, gagging him tightly with his bandanna. Jed had fetched along plenty of rawhide lengths; he'd given some to Huck but there were enough left so that Nelson could hogtie Jed. The spare thongs had no doubt been intended for the inside guards.

He grunted, cursing to himself at the strain of hoisting the heavy Jed back into the buggy. Laramie roped him in place, in the driver's seat, climbed in beside the unconscious man and waited. Jed began moaning; Laramie clipped him again and Jed subsided.

Soon, Huck came slipping through the shadows. "Jed, I reckon I busted his neck, but I got him. And I hid him good."

Laramie slipped down, close to Huck, who craned forward as he stared, surprised, at Jed in the dark interior of the buggy. His back was turned toward Nelson, who quickly buffaloed him, then gagged and tied Huck and added him to the collection.

He was puffing from exertion and the closeness of the operation; he'd had to play it as it came, just as he'd figured he would. It had been a tossup, whether he could succeed, for both Jed and Huck were tough fighters.

He squeezed Jed over against Huck, untied the horse, then got into the driver's seat, and slapped the reins on the animal's rump.

After a short run he pulled up in front of the small house Brock Peters had rented for the Pinkertons' use while in Fort Smith. He hoped Peters would be there; it was always possible Brock might have gone off on a short mission, though he'd promised to be on hand when

Laramie got back from the Nations.

He checked his two captives, made sure their bonds were tight; both were mumbling, half-conscious, behind the gags.

Tying the horse to the hitchpost out front, Nelson trotted to the front door and tried the latch, but it was bolted inside, so he began banging on it with his gun butt. He was relieved when he saw a light come on inside; somebody inside had touched off a lamp.

A minute later, Peters came and unbolted the door. He had on a loose shirt and had pulled his pants on hastily; his feet were bare.

"Where in blue blazes you been!" demanded Peters, annoyed at having been roused from a peaceful sleep.

Laramie pushed in past him. A small lamp burned on the parlor table and there was a bottle of whiskey near it. Nelson grabbed the latter and took a satisfying pull on it, as Brock Peters went on scolding him. "What you been doin', foolin' with some Cherokee princess over in the Nations?"

"Oh, sure," said Laramie, taking another swig. There was an open box of cigars on the table and he took one, bit off an end, and lit up. "I got no time for palaver, Brock. Get my credentials, fetch your own and don't forget your hogleg. A shotgun would be a help, too. Hustle, dang it. I'll fill you in later." The tone of his voice stopped Brock from further chitchat. "Meet me outside," ordered Laramie. "I got two prisoners I don't want to lose."

He trotted back to the buggy. Jed and Huck had managed to rub the gags off their mouths, and were squirming around as they struggled to loosen the ties.

"Sit quiet, gents," drawled Laramie, cocking his revolver and holding it on them.

60

Jed began cursing him in a virulent monotone, while Huck added some fancy touches. "You'll die for this, and hard, Laramie," promised Jed.

"I'm a Pinkerton, boys," said Laramie easily, shifting the cigar in his teeth. "Have patience. You'll have plenty of time to think things over in Judge Parker's calaboose." The Fort Smith jail was known far and wide as "Hell on the Border."

Brock Peters came hurrying out. He'd pulled on his boots and set his derby hat on his curly hair. He had strapped on a cartridge belt with his Colt revolver, and carried a sawed-off shotgun under one arm.

"First we got to get rid of these prisoners, Brock. They're both wanted for murder—or maybe we should make it 'murders.' Jed and Huck, like you to meet my boss, Brock Peters of the Pinkertons."

"I reckon Judge Parker 'll be happy to see 'em," nodded Peters. Ignoring the purple cursing of the captives, he added, "Ain't room in there for me, Laramie. I'll saddle up pronto and catch you at the lockup."

Laramie got in and set off. He drew up before the big building; Police headquarters was on one side, on the other wing was the famous Judge Isaac C. Parker's courtroom. In the basement was a dismal, huge chamber with small barred windows where prisoners awaiting trial were held, guarded day and night by armed jailers. So far, nobody had escaped, except to be led in chains to the court for trial, or on disposal of his case, to the gallows in the yard; if lucky, the criminal might be sent to a federal penitentiary. "Hell on the Border" was no joke.

Nelson jumped down, and saw, limned against the moonsky, the high, wide gallows where a dozen men could be dropped at once to eternity. It gave even Laramie a shiver to see this machine of death.

A jailer sang out, "Hey, you! What you want, this time of night?" He had a shotgun at the ready.

"I'm a Pinkerton," replied Laramie. "Got a couple prisoners for you, prize ones."

Brock Peters came riding up on the pinto he'd hired for use in Fort Smith.

They saw the captives charged at the desk; the officers in command knew Peters, and Brock had his own as well as Laramie's credentials. Soon, Jed and Huck, hand-cuffed, were led off to the lockup.

"Tie your horse behind and get in by me," said Laramie, as they left the police station. "We got more work to do." It was pleasant to issue orders to the boss.

Nelson knew he had to capture Lance or the bandit would go back and warn Mazzotti. And he wished to pick up Wingfoot. As they rolled south toward the spot on the river where Eagleclaw waited, Laramie quickly told Peters what had happened in the Nations.

"We better go see Judge Parker," said Brock.

"First we snaffle this Injun and Lance. I don't want to lose Wingfoot, and we don't want word to get back to Mazzotti or any of the men with him."

They left the buggy and Brock's pinto in the woods. Laramie led the way down to the river bank; the skiff was drawn up as it had been left. Nelson called, "Eagleclaw! C'mon, we go back."

Eagleclaw materialized from the shadows. "Jed?" he asked.

"He's comin'," replied Laramie, and then the Indian gasped as he found himself staring into the black muzzle of Nelson's Colt.

He signalled Peters, who joined them. "Take the oars,

62

Eagleclaw," ordered Laramie. "You balk or sing out, you're dead."

The Indian sullenly picked up the sweeps and rowed them across the stream; the skiff grounded on the west bank. Nelson left Eagleclaw in Brock's care and hurried through the trees. "That you, Jed?" said Lance.

"It's Laramie. Jed and Huck 're fetchin' the loot. I was able to open that safe."

"Bueno. I was gettin' worried."

Lance turned his back to untie the horses and have them ready. Nelson rammed his sixgun into the man's spine. "Reach high, Lance. You're under arrest. Pinkerton!"

"What the—" Lance was completely flustered.

"You heard, I'm a Pinkerton. Jed and Huck are locked up in Parker's jail. You'll join 'em."

With a frantic curse, Lance whirled, trying to knock up Laramie's revolver with his left arm as he went for his own weapon. Laramie had to pull trigger; the explosion of the heavy Colt echoed in the forest. The horses danced, jerking at their tethers.

Lance's pistol had gone off; the bullet drove into the dirt, and Lance collapsed. As Laramie knelt to check on him, Brock Peters came tearing through the trees, shotgun cocked and ready.

"You all right, Laramie?"

"I am, but Lance ain't. He's cashed in. Where's that Injun?"

"Handcuffed to a limb."

Laramie untied Wingfoot; they hurried back, Nelson leading his horse the short distance. Peters freed Eagleclaw, who got into the skiff and took the oars. Brock held a gun on him; Laramie lengthened his rein and fastened an end to a tie ring. The animal would swim in the boat's wake. As for Lance's body and the other mounts, Fort Smith officers could go over and take care of that.

Sullen and silent, Eagleclaw rowed them to the Arkansas shore.

Turning the Indian over at the lockup, the two rode to Judge Isaac Parker's home. Parker was one of the most famous jurists in the country; his job was to bring law and order to the western district of Arkansas, which included the lawless Indian Territory.

The small home was dark, but after Peters had jangled the doorbell a few times, a light showed, and soon a tall, well-fleshed man with a brown goatee and mustache opened the door; he was a most impressive figure, a stern but impartial magistrate. Many threats had been made against Parker's life but he was utterly fearless.

"What is it, this time of night?" he demanded. He raised the small lamp higher so he could see the visitors' faces. "Oh, it's you, Mr. Peters. What have the Pinkertons found out?"

"Plenty, Judge Parker. This is Laramie Nelson, my best operative. I told you I'd sent him into the Nations, and he's got a mighty good story to tell you."

VIII

With Tolliver and Smythe, two of Parker's tough deputy marshals, Laramie Nelson approached the main village of the Osage Nation.

He'd slept a few hours in Brock's house in town, as preparations had been completed for the raid on Ferdinand Mazzotti's stronghold.

"Remember, Pinkerton," said Tolliver, a sturdy, blunt

officer with touches of grizzly hair at his temples, "the Indians'll obey their chief. But the medicine man—we call him Kat-a-tillee, close as we can come to pronouncin' his outlandish name—he tells the chief what to do. You keep shut and let me'n Smythe do the spielin'."

Laramie was glad to oblige. He knew several of the western tribes' languages as well as the universal sign talk, but wasn't acquainted with the Osage. There were literally hundreds of differing tongues among the redskins.

They reached a large clearing and were challenged by a pack of baying mongrel dogs. Tepees and wood-and-brush shacks stood around the perimeter. Old men squatted in the shade, smoking their pipes and talking of past glories. Small naked children frollicked about, playing at hunting and tug-of-war. Squaws worked industriously, cooking at outdoor hearths, mending clothing. Some of the braves wore white man's garb, and all stared at the visitors.

The dogs went yelping off as larger boys, on order, pelted them with stones.

A tall, muscular brave approached. "Howdy, Rudolph," sang out Tolliver. Smythe said in a low voice, "Most of 'em got Christian names, besides their Indian ones."

Rudolph waved, evidently inviting the visitors to dismount. Tolliver got down, Laramie and Smythe followed his example. An Osage lad, with arrow-straight back, took Tolliver's rein, while others courteously held Wingfoot and Smythe's animal.

Tolliver spoke fluent Osage to Rudolph, who nodded, and the three trailed the brave to a more pretentious structure. "Chief Wahnonaw's lodge," Smythe said to Laramie.

Soon an impressive figure emerged and gravely shook hands with Tolliver, who had fetched along gifts, cigarettes, plug tobacco, trinkets, which he presented to the chief. They squatted in the shade, smoking and talking together. Laramie listened as they palavered, many gestures accompanying the words.

Wahnowna kept shaking his head. But finally he shrugged and nodded, rose and led Tolliver to a tepee set close to the surrounding forest. It was covered with strange designs, while at one side was a hearth with a pile of round stones by it and what looked like a movable enclosed framework. "Sweat hut," explained Smythe. "Medicine man heats them stones and tosses 'em into a kettle of water in the box. Sweats hell out of a sick person or one possessed by an evil spirit."

Laramie could see through the open doorway of the tepee. The chief sang out, and a tall, skeleton-thin Indian clad in rich otter skins and a bizarre headdress appeared. "That's Kat-a-tillee," said Smythe to Laramie.

Wahnonaw spoke to the medicine man, who signalled. Tolliver went in, but the chief, Laramie and Smythe waited outside. The two white men sat down in the shade and smoked, and the marshal told Nelson, "Kat-a-tillee's a miserly old rascal. He knows the value of our money, and if Tolliver slipped him that fat roll your pal Brock Peters supplied, maybe Kat-a-tillee'll agree to lift the spell off the Cave of the Spirits. He'll tell the Chief to send his fightin' men with us."

Laramie Nelson, Tolliver and Smythe led the way toward the crest. Behind them came a large band of Osage warriors, armed with carbines and knives; a few had bows and quivers of arrows over their muscular shoulders. For a fat fee, Kat-a-tillee had ceremoniously taken the curse

66

off the caverns, temporarily. The medicine man had declared that until the moon again rose full, the spirits of the dead would lie quiet.

Laramie had been astonished at the change in the Osage braves. In nondescript white man's clothes, they hadn't looked like much. But dressed and painted for war, they were most impressive.

They had shaved their heads except for long topknots held by snake bands; naked to the waist, their powerful torsos gleamed with bear grease, muscles standing out, and their strong legs were cased in deerskin leggings. They sure looked like ace fighting men, and Laramie felt a deep admiration for them; he could see why the Osage had once been mighty warriors, feared by other tribes.

Osage scouts had led them swiftly and directly to the ridge on the north of the valley, while others had guided Brock Peters, Judge Parker's chief marshal and his fighting men through the wilderness to the gate on the east.

Tolliver whispered to a brave; the subchief and three lithe warriors snaked to the track along which the mounted sentry would patrol. Before long, they caught the sound of approaching hoofbeats, and then saw the rider framed against the sky.

Hardly a sound was made as a big Indian leaped on the horse, a sinewy arm winding around the startled white man's neck.

Another caught the alarmed horse's bridle and pulled him down as he reared; a third held the beast's nostrils so he couldn't sound off. The fourth Osage helped unseat and subdue the outlaw. In a jiffy, the prisoner was gagged and bound.

Laramie knew the location of the screened slide down

to the rear caves; so did some of the Osage. Nelson went first, descending carefully so as not to dislodge pebbles and gravel; the Indians seemed able to see in the gloom, like cats. Tolliver, Smythe, more braves came down.

As Nelson stood, listening, he heard gunfire break out from the east narrows; it was dulled by the cavern walls, but it grew heavy. Laramie knew what that was: Brock Peters and the force, while they must not try to rush that deadly gap till it was made safe by a rear attack, were to distract Riley's guards, keep them busy while Laramie, Tolliver and the Osage crept up from behind.

Laramie turned off toward Nora's small side cave. He wanted to make sure she wasn't harmed. The girl lay asleep on her bed, a lamp turned low against the rock wall. Nelson put a hand over her mouth and she gave a muffled, startled cry. He whispered, "It's me, Laramie, Nora. I've come back. Keep quiet. I want to help you."

Sitting by her, he kissed her. "Laramie—what—?" she stammered.

"Sit tight, Nora. I'm really a Pinkerton detective. We aim to smash this den of killers and robbers."

He could see shadowy figures slipping past, headed for the main front cavern. A pistol shot banged, echoing from Mazzotti's grotto. Nora gasped. "Please don't hurt my uncle!" she begged. She began to sob.

"Nora, I got to leave but I'll be back."

Deputy Marshal Smythe turned over and joined them.

"Here's the young lady I told you about, Smythe," said Nelson. "Do like I asked, stand by her and make sure she ain't bothered." Smythe nodded; he had a sawed-off shotgun firmly in his hand.

Laramie drew his Colt and padded off. As he reached the big front cavern, he saw that Mazzotti's curtain had been ripped down. Tolliver and several Indians stood by the Emperor's bed. Tolliver had a bull's-eye lantern and in its beam, the marshal stood, staring at the unmoving, strange figure on the couch.

Ferdinand Mazzotti lay, his bald head a bloody mess.

"He had a derringer under his pillow," growled Tolliver. "Blew out his brains when I told him he was under arrest!"

Laramie shook his head; it would be a blow for Nora, but maybe it was better than having her uncle hung on Judge Parker's gallows.

The battle was increasing in fury, outside, and Laramie rushed on out and down to the level. Indian braves were flitting through the big camp; here and there, startled outlaws were firing at the shadowy figures, but were soon silenced.

In a short interval, the main section was under control; a few bandits on the far side of the creek had managed to seize horses and were riding hell-for-leather toward the western end of the long valley.

Laramie and Tolliver marshalled as many Osage braves as they could summon, hustling toward the gate. When Peters and his crew had opened up outside the narrows, Riley and most of his guards had hurried to the gap.

Guns bellowed, flashed yellow in the night, as Colonel Riley directed the defense at the gate. The enemy's attention was on the force to the east and did not see the swift approach of the Indians, Laramie and Tolliver with them. Several Osage warriors were hit, but as Laramie had figured, Riley's army was panicked.

When they had subdued the defenders on the bluffs, Tolliver fired prearranged signal shots in the air, and sang out to Brock Peters, the chief marshal and his deputies, who had taken cover just east of the narrows.

A number of Riley's men had surrendered as they saw they were done for, but the colonel himself was dead, riddled with lead. The prisoners would be arraigned in Judge Parker's courtroom in Fort Smith, and the gallows would be very busy after the trials...

Puffing for wind, Laramie Nelson went over to the creek to wash; a bullet had cut a hunk of flesh from his left forearm, another had burned one bronzed cheek. After cleaning it, he bound the arm wounds; it could be given better treatment later.

Brock Peters and the chief marshal came riding into the valley, at the head of their aides. Big bonfires were touched off, and soon order was restored, prisoners secured and under guard.

Laramie went back into the caverns, and to Nora; Smythe had watched over the girl as the battle raged.

"Nora," said Nelson, "your uncle's dead. He shot himself, rather than be arrested. You come back to civilization with us."

She began sobbing again, and he sought to comfort her. At last he was able to control her, and she said, "All right, Laramie. I'll go—if you'll promise to stay with me."

"I sure will," he said, and, bending down, kissed her.

She was mighty pretty and sweet. Laramie meant to stay in Fort Smith long enough to make sure she was put in school and would be cared for by a decent family; Judge Parker would surely help.

He knew Brock Peters always had another "easy" assignment for Laramie to work on, one that must be undertaken at once if not sooner. A simple job, like smashing the Emperor of the Nations and his gang.

70

But Laramie intended to remain in Fort Smith for a while, ensuring Nora would enjoy a chance at real happiness. He'd squire her around and show her the sights, it would be a pleasure.

He'd earned a respite, so he'd let Brock Peters rave and rant and move on when he, Laramie Nelson, was ready to travel again.

TRAIL HERD TO ABILENE

I

Over the hum of the ever-present Kansas wind and the rumble of many thousand hooves was heard the angry crack of a rifle shot. A rangy longhorn steer in the front rank went down on his face, drilled neatly between the eyes. For several minutes it was touch and go whether the easily spooked longhorns would stampede, but the experienced trail hands managed to keep them under control.

Only after they got the herd quieted down could the trail drivers turn their attention to the mounted men who blocked their path along the cattle trail. They were a hard-bitten, ragtag bunch, many wearing scraps of old Confederate uniforms. The trail boss rode out ahead to meet them.

"What the hell's the idea?" he demanded.

The spokesman for the mounted men was a stringy, weathered individual, brown mustache stained with tobacco juice. He said harshly, "Where you think you're takin' them steers, cowboy?"

"The stockyards in Abilene."

"Think again, cowboy. Ain't no sick Texas cattle comin' into Kansas. Now you just get that herd turned around and outa here or the next one of you to eat prairie dirt won't.be no steer."

For a long and dangerous moment the Texas drovers and the Kansas men confronted each other. The cowboys were rough men, and not the kind to back off from a gun battle. However, they were not fools. Outnumbered nearly ten to one, and out-gunned by the rifle-carrying blockaders, they finally turned the herd around and headed it back south.

This was the story as Laramie Nelson heard it in a Chicago hotel room from Brock Peters, his Pinkerton boss. A third man in the room, wearing a black brush of a beard and an earnest look in his eyes, had been introduced to Laramie as Joseph G. McCoy, a cattle shipper from Springfield, who had recently built the new Abilene stockyards.

Laramie had sat listening impassively while the other men did the talking. Now he stood, stretching his long legs, and strolled to the windows, where he stared out at Chicago, washed clean by an October rain. Lake Michigan sparkled in the distance. Deep in thought, Laramie rolled a cigarette and took a deep drag.

Finally he turned and regarded the others out of slightly squinted gray eyes that had looked for long hours into the prairie sun. "On the face of it, the trouble seems to be over. You say these drovers ran into an armed gang of some sort, so they turned around and headed back. But I know you didn't bring me all the way up here from New

76

Mexico to investigate the shooting of a steer, so there must be more to it."

"There is, Laramie," Brock Peters said. "There's a lot more to it." Peters was a small man, dandified in Eastern clothes, with the innocent face of a church elder. However, beneath the mild outward appearance was a man capable of swift and deadly action when the need was there. "The trouble out in Abilene is just beginning, and what it amounts to is dangerously close to an act of war. Those drovers didn't take that herd back to Texas. They're camped right now just north of the Cottonwood River, waiting. Waiting for reinforcements, would be my guess. When they get them, they'll drive those cattle north again, and there will be more killing than we've seen since the end of the war."

"Just who are these blockaders, and what are they after?" Laramie asked.

"I'll let Mr. McCoy answer that," Peters replied. "He's just back from Abilene."

"As near as I have been able to learn," McCoy said, "most of the band are ex-guerrillas who were with Quantrill. They're a dangerous, blood-thirsty bunch, and they're running free and wild around Abilene right now. It appears they're being paid by an association of farmers and ranchers around there. The nestors are afraid that the Texas cattle will bring in the ticks that cause Texas fever. The longhorns themselves are immune to the disease, but they're carriers and the ticks they carry can infect the cows, oxen and cattle around Abilene."

"Are the farmers right about the Texas steers carrying ticks?" Laramie asked.

McCoy met his gaze levelly. "Yes."

Laramie drawled, "Then it seems to me the people who

77

want to keep them out have a pretty good case."

"Yes, they have a case," McCoy admitted readily. "But there are a couple of points I think you should consider. First, although we know there are ticks on these cattle, we have no real reason to believe they are the kind that carry the fever. Second, Texas cattle will go north to Chicago on the railroad. If not through Abilene, then through Salina to the west or Junction City to the east. It's progress, gentlemen, and right or wrong, it's not going to be stopped. But the most important consideration right now is that if this blockade isn't broken, and broken soon, a lot of people are going to die."

Laramie nodded thoughtfully. "I see what you mean."

McCoy pulled a watch from his vest. He said, "If you gentlemen will excuse me, I'm due at a committee hearing. I trust I will be seeing you both again."

"I trust you will," said Brock Peters.

They shook hands all around, and McCoy left the hotel room.

The moment they were alone, Peters said, "How does it size up to you, Laramie?"

"I'd say there's more going on in Abilene than we've been told about. It's not likely the farmers, at least none I've ever known, would get together and hire a gang of cutthroats like Quantrill's men to do their dirty work for them. There's got to be something or somebody stirring up trouble."

"That's what I think," Peters said. "I want you to go to Abilene and see what you can ferret out. If possible, head off the trouble before it turns into a war. But don't try to make like a one-man army!"

"Now would I do that?" Laramie drawled, showing Peters one of his rare smiles.

"You might, you have before. The man who will meet you at the train depot is Harlan Vane. He's connected with the railroad, and has organized the Abilene businessmen. He'll be friendly to you, because the economic future of Abilene hinges on bringing the trail herds to the stockyards there. One man you'll want to see is Stanley Forrest. He has the biggest ranch in the area, and he won't be so friendly, since he's considered the leader of the ranchers determined to keep Texas cattle out of Kansas."

"No disguise this time?"

"We couldn't work it, even if we wanted to," Peters said. "Too many people in Abilene know you're coming. This time you'll just be exactly what you are, a Pinkerton agent acting on behalf of the people who want to get the cattle through." Peters pulled a thick, yellow envelope from his coat pocket. "Here's your train ticket and expense money. As usual, I'll want a full accounting of every nickel you spend."

"As usual," Laramie drawled with a spare grin.

"And if you need to contact me for anything, I'll be in my Denver office."

II

The train rolled into Abilene past the hundred-car siding built by the Kansas Pacific at the urging of Joseph McCoy. Next to the siding were the freshly-built loading and feeding pens, standing empty, where the cattle would be kept before they were loaded into cars bound for Chicago.

If the cattle ever got this far.

The train slowed with a hiss of steam up front and grinding squeal of brakes. Through the sooty window of his coach car, Laramie Nelson saw the unfinished three-story Drover's Cottage. This would be the most magnificent structure in western Kansas and would house the cowboys, the cattle buyers, the bankers, the businessmen, and countless others who would be drawn to Abilene when the great trail herds arrived.

If they ever arrived.

As the cars came to a clanking stop, Laramie pulled his bag from beneath the wicker seat, walked the length of the nearly empty car, and swung down to the platform. A goodly number of Abilene citizens had turned out to see the train pull in. This was still a special event in their town, it being much more common for the K. P. to highball right on through, not even slowing down to snatch a mailbag or throw one off.

A stout man in a black frock coat and gray vest shouldered his way through the crowd. He looked freshly barbered and powdered, and he wore an air of importance like a cloak.

"Laramie Nelson?" the man said. "I'm Harlan Vane."

Laramie shook Vane's hand, which was uncallused and moist.

"I'm surely glad you're here," Vane said. "Things are getting out of hand more every day. I thought we'd go right to my office and I'll fill you in on what's happening."

"If it's all the same to you," Laramie responded, "I'd like to freshen up a bit first. That was a long and dusty ride."

"Yes, of course," Vane said. "There's a room reserved for you over at the hotel. I just thought that the sooner we could get down to business, the better."

"I agree, Mr. Vane. Come on along and we can talk while I clean up."

Harlan Vane had to hurry to keep up with the longer strides of the Pinkerton man as they crossed the dusty street and headed for the two-story wood frame structure that was obviously the hotel. Although Laramie appeared to be taking little notice of the people on the street, his gray eyes missed nothing. There were a large number of roughhewn men, carelessly shaven and heavily armed, who didn't belong among the farmers and merchants of a Kansas town.

Even those who were drunk, and quite a few seemed to be, walked with the careful-footed tread and wary-eyed look of the guerrilla. These, then, might be the ex-Quantrill men who were manning the blockade against the Texas trail herds. To Laramie, they were so many kegs of black powder, ready to be ignited by a careless spark.

The walls of Laramie's hotel room were bare wood. The furniture consisted of a narrow metal frame bed, a single chair, and a dresser that had once been enameled white. On the dresser was a basin of cold water. Laramie stripped to the waist and splashed water over his face and shoulder, scouring his skin with the gritty soap provided by the hotel.

"It's not the most deluxe accomodations," Vane apologized. "Nothing at all like the Drover's Cottage will be when it's finally finished."

"I've stayed in a lot worse," Laramie said.

"Yes, we all have. Now, here's what I have planned for you," Vane said, ticking off the points on his fingertips, talking at a fast clip. "First, you'll come with me to a meeting of the local businessmen's committee. I'm the chairman, by the way. These men will fill you in on all the economic reasons why this blockade must be broken—the future prosperity of Abilene, that sort of thing. I'm

81

sure you're aware of most of these things, but we want to be damn sure that we all know.

"I'm afraid the law here won't be much help to you, Nelson. We have a sheriff of sorts, but he usually manages to be somewhere else whenever trouble pops up. As a last resort, I thought we could call on troops from Fort Riley. But before that we'll get together a delegation of local merchants and pay a call on Stanley Forrest. He seems to be the leader of the troublemaking element hereabouts. Then we'll—"

"Whoa, hoss, whoa up!" Laramie held up a hand. "You shouldn't have gone to all that trouble for me, Mr. Vane. Making all those plans. I don't work that way."

Vane was taken aback. "What do you mean?"

Laramie turned back to the clouded mirror and resumed lathering his lean face. "I mean I like to move around by myself and get the feel of a job before I jump into anything. It's been my experience that following another man's laid-out plans can get a man into an awful lot of trouble."

"I only thought it would save time," Vane said in an injured tone. "And if you saw those men hanging around the streets, you know time is not on our side."

"I appreciate that, Mr. Vane, and I'll be in touch with you."

Harlan Vane stood up, cleared his throat several times, looked at his watch and finally said uncertainly, "Well, I'd better report to the committee. I'll see you later?"

"Later," Laramie drawled, drawing the razor down along his jaw.

Vane started to say something else, then scowled blackly and went out the door.

When Laramie Nelson had rinsed away most of the

82

travel grit and scraped off his stubble, he pulled on his clean clothes, buckled on his gunbelt and headed downstairs.

He pushed through the door and swung down the street toward a building with a tall false front, a faded sign identifying it as the Bull's Head Saloon. Before he had gone twenty yards Laramie knew without turning to look that a growing crowd of the ex-Quantrill men had fallen in behind him. Laramie neither slowed nor quickened his pace, but his wrist brushed against the stock of his Colt, checking the reassuringly familiar position of the pistol.

"Hey, you!" one of the men called harshly. "Mister Pinkerton!"

Laramie stopped and turned slowly to face the men. "You talking to me?" he drawled.

One of the ragged crowd took a step out ahead of the others. He was a beefy man with a whiskey flush and a dangerous glint in his eyes. He said, "What are you doing in them Western clothes, Mister Pinkerton? Trying to fool folks into thinkin' you're a real man?"

Laramie knew he was being baited. It was the beginning of a deadly pattern he knew well. A schoolboy taunt from one grown man to another is answered in kind. The insults grow cruder and the challenges stronger until the men must go for iron and one of them must die.

Laramie had no wish to kill this man. Not only would it be a senseless death, but it would make his job that much more difficult. And yet he couldn't back down. A man who showed cowardice in one fight would soon find a dozen more waiting for him with bullies anxious to prove their manhood at his expense.

Laramie chose to do the unexpected. With no change of expression he moved in a casual, loose-jointed stride straight for the man who had taunted him. The man watched Laramie come with open-mouthed bewilderment. This was not part of the ritual. So confused was that he forgot to reach for the gun strapped around his waist. His companions fell silent, waiting to see what would develop.

They didn't have long to wait. With his gaze never leaving the other man's face, Laramie walked directly up to him and smashed his right fist into the solar plexus. The beefy man doubled forward as much from surprise as from the force of the blow.

"That answer your question, friend?" Laramie asked.

With a bellow of rage the man straightened up, and Laramie hit him twice more, one a clubbing blow just below the ear and once on the point of the chin. The man crashed to the dirt. He tried groggily to get to his feet, but fell back.

For several heartbeats the tension was thick as the Kansas dust. If the fallen man went for his gun, Laramie would have to kill him. He would have no choice. And if his friends decided to take up the fight, Laramie would be far outnumbered. These were ruthless men, thieves and killers, but there was one thing about them that Laramie was counting on now. They had been soldiers. Even soldiers of Quantrill's ruthless band should have somewhere within them, however twisted, a sense of honor.

The man on the ground levered himself up to a sitting position and worked his jaw from side to side with his hand. His eyes slowly lost their glaze, and he focused on Laramie. "Okay, Pinkerton, you win. This time."

The men who had been watching suddenly became

intent on other business and wandered away in twos and threes. There was no friendship in the glances they shot Laramie Nelson but there was a new respect. Laramie turned his back on them and continued on his way to the Bull's Head Saloon.

The bar in the Bull's Head was of a dark, heavy wood, not the ornate, highly polished mahogany found farther east, but better than the rough planking used in some frontier saloons. Laramie ordered a glass of whiskey, took a couple of hardboiled eggs from a bowl on the bar, and carried them to a table against a side wall.

At the bar a few local farmers and a couple of cowpunchers glanced at him with mild interest, then returned to their desultory drinking. A piano stood dusty and silent at the far end of the room. At one table a gambler in a frock coat and a gray planter's hat sat alone, idly shuffling a deck of cards, waiting patiently for the action to pick up.

A movement at the door drew Laramie's attention. A narrow-shouldered man in his middle twenties stood in the doorway scanning the customers inside. He was hatless, and his pale hair was combed to one side, flat against his head. Now his gaze settled on Laramie, and he came quickly to his table.

"Laramie Nelson?" he asked.

"That's right."

"I'm Jesse Forrest."

"Have a seat." Laramie motioned. "I've heard of a Stanley Forrest. Any kin?"

"Stanley Forrest married my mother." Jesse pulled out the chair opposite Laramie and perched on the edge of it. "I was watching, I saw the way you handled that ruckus outside in the street. That was well done."

Laramie nodded slightly, but said nothing, waiting for the young man to continue.

"I just want you to know that I was ready to help you if the shooting had started."

"Now why would you have done that?" Laramie said in astonishment.

Jesse looked around, as though looking for possible eavesdroppers. There was no one closer than two tables away.

"I know why you're in town," he said in a low voice. "It's to break the blockade and let those Texas cattle through. That's what I want too. It's best for Abilene in the long run."

"I heard that Stanley Forrest was one of the leaders of those wanting to keep the herds out," Laramie said.

Jesse made a wry face. "My stepfather and I don't always agree. But he does have a lot of influence with the ranchers and farmers around here. I expect you'd like to meet him?"

"I would."

Jesse leaned across the table to say eagerly, "Then come on out to our place for supper tonight. Maybe you can talk some sense into the old man. He sure won't listen to me."

"Well, now, how do I know your stepfather will approve of my coming?"

"Oh, it was his idea, for a different reason. He told me to ask you. He wants to talk you into staying out of it."

"All right then," Laramie said. "I'd appreciate a home-cooked meal."

"Fine, fine. Our place is three miles south of town, just off the main road. You can't miss it." Jesse put both hands on the table and levered himself up. "I'd better get going. I left my stepsister out in front of the dressmaker's, and she's not a girl likes to be kept waiting."

"I'll walk out with you," Laramie said.

The two men left the saloon and crossed the street to where a slim girl of about twenty sat in a buckboard. Her hair was a rich chestnut, her eyes brown and alert.

"Stella, this is Laramie Nelson," Jesse said.

"Oh, the Pinkerton agent," the girl said with an audible sniff of disapproval. "How do you do?"

Laramie doffed his hat. "Hello, Miss Forrest."

"Mr. Nelson will be having supper with us tonight, Stella," Jesse said.

"How nice. I'll look forward to talking to you, Mr. Nelson."

"Likewise, I'm sure," Laramie said gravely. He was sure he saw a flicker of a smile on the girl's lips as Jesse snapped the reins and sent the buckboard clattering up the street.

III

All that remained of daylight was a crimson glow low in the west as Laramie Nelson cantered south along the road out of Abilene. He was riding a rented pinto. He missed his own horse, Wingfoot, but Brock Peters' summons had been so urgent he'd had to leave the animal in New Mexico.

Most of the settlers who had come to the area had established their farms along the bottomland next to the Smoky Hill River. The houses Laramie saw before darkness set in were mostly rough log structures, with a few green wood outbuildings.

The horse Laramie had hired was far past his colthood

days, but he was still sound and willing, a better bargain than a man usually found in a livery stable. He forded the shallow river with a sure step and climbed the easy slope of the opposite bank to where the trail led through a clump of cottonwoods.

Along with the rustle of dry limbs in the wind came a soft, metallic sound that didn't belong. As Laramie reined in abruptly to listen again, a rifle cracked to his left, the bullet racketing into the woods on his other side. Laramie vaulted from the saddle without a second's thought and hit the ground, using the flat of his hand to break the fall. He rolled over and over into the low brush. Then he stopped, quiet as death. His Colt was gripped in his hand.

The horse, startled when his driver leaped off, had bolted several yards down the trail, where he now stood snorting and dancing nervously. Laramie could see nothing in the dark woods across from him. After several moments there was a crackling of dry brush and the sound of running footsteps going away. Then came the creak of leather and a muted jangle of metal as someone mounted a horse. Hoofbeats faded rapidly into the sound of the wind as the unseen rider galloped away.

Laramie stood up and holstered his revolver. His palm was moist and slippery. He wiped it on his trouser leg and walked slowly along the trail to the pinto, speaking to the animal in a low, soothing voice. The old horse stood quivering until Laramie was mounted up.

It was full dark by the time he reached the Forrest place. The main house was a two-story frame structure, sturdier and more comfortable-looking than the other houses he had seen along the way. Lamplight glowed warm and inviting in the downstairs windows.

As Laramie dismounted, the front door opened, and a

powerful man with steely gray hair and a leathery, crag-like face clumped out onto the porch.

"Evening," the man said.

"Howdy. I'm Laramie Nelson."

"I figured as much. We've been expecting you, Mr. Nelson. I'm Stanley Forrest. Come on in."

"I'd like to see to my horse first."

Forrest squinted around in the darkness. "There should be a hand here to take care of that. They're never around when you want them." He made a megaphone of his hands and bellowed toward one of the outbuildings. "Pete!"

Jesse Forrest walked out onto the porch behind his stepfather.

"Hello, Laramie," he said, and to Forrest, "Never mind, I'll help Laramie stable his horse."

"If you'll just show me the way, I can manage," Laramie said.

Jesse batted a hand at him. "Back in a minute." He disappeared into the house, finally returning with a glowing lantern.

As they walked toward a solid wooden building bulking large in the dark, Laramie brushed at some of the trail dirt on his clothing with the back of his hand.

"What happened?" Jesse asked. "Have an accident?"

"You might say that, yeah. I ran into a bushwhacker in the cottonwood grove down by the river. He took a shot at me and I dived from the dirt."

"The hell you say!" Jesse stopped short, holding up the lantern to look closely at Laramie.

"No real harm done," Laramie said. "He missed both me and my horse. Either a bad shot or he just wanted to warn me off."

"You don't suppose it was that fellow you knocked down outside the Bull's Head?"

"It's possible," Laramie said.

They entered the barn and led the pinto past the docile gray Laramie had seen hitched to the buckboard in town earlier and a glistening bay gelding draped with a blanket.

Laramie patted the gelding's sleek neck as they passed. "Nice looking hoss."

"Stella's," Jesse said shortly. "She's the real horseman in this family."

They left the pinto in an empty stall, saw to it that he had grain and strolled back to the house.

Stanley Forrest, Stella, and Forrest's wife, Emma, were waiting for them. Emma, Laramie later learned, was Forrest's second wife, married after the death of Stella's mother, and Jesse's mother. She was a frail woman, thin as a fence post, and almost never spoke unless spoken to first.

"Somebody tried to bushwhack Laramie on his way here tonight," Jesse announced as soon as the introductions were over.

"How awful!" Stella exclaimed. "Who would do a thing like that?"

"We think it was one of those ex-Quantrill men Laramie had a run-in with earlier in town," Jesse said.

"I couldn't say that for sure," Laramie said. "It was too dark to see anything, and I didn't get a good look at whoever it was."

Stella said, "You seem awfully calm for a man who's just been shot at."

"It's happened before." Laramie shrugged. "It goes with the job."

Stella appraised Laramie carefully.

"I suppose your work does involve a lot of shooting and bloodshed." Her voice was hostile. "I only hope you haven't brought it to Abilene with you."

"My main purpose in being here, Miss Forrest, is to try and head off any shooting and bloodshed."

"Come, come, Stella," Forrest chided. "Let's at least feed our guest before we start talking business."

"Of course, father. I am sorry. Will you forgive me, Laramie?" She smiled. "It is all right, isn't it, if we start using first names?"

"You're forgiven, and first names are fine with me."

"Good!" With her bright smile spreading, she took Laramie's arm and led the way through a dark-beamed archway into the dining room.

The table was set with crisp white linen and silver that gleamed softly in the candlelight. The food, prepared and served by Emma Forrest, wasn't elaborate, but it was very good. When Laramie told Mrs. Forrest truthfully that it was the best meal he'd eaten in months, she blushed and disappeared into the kitchen for an apple cobbler dessert.

Following dinner, Forrest poured brandy for the men in the parlor. The rancher offered Laramie a cigar, which he refused. Forrest took one himself and lit it, while Laramie built a cigarette. Emma Forrest was busy in the kitchen, but Stella soon joined the men in the parlor, showing no signs of self-consciousness. Although Jesse seemed ill-at-ease about his stepsister's presence, Forrest accepted her into the group without hesitation. Even, Laramie noticed, with a touch of pride.

"Suppose you begin, Nelson," Forest said, "by explaining your purpose in Abilene."

"I'm here on the behalf of Joseph McCoy. I think you know him."

"Yes. I have always found Mr. McCoy to be a gentleman. However, his goals for the future of Abilene and Kansas are different from mine."

"And your goals are to keep Texas cattle out?"

"My goals and that of others hereabouts are to protect our own stock from Texas fever. We all know the disease is caused by the ticks that these Texas longhorns carry."

"There is a cattle disease that is caused by ticks," Laramie admitted. "In Texas, by the way, they call it Spanish fever. But you can't be sure the cattle you're turning back now are carrying the ticks."

"Can't be sure they're not, either," Forrest snapped.

"But there's the future of Abilene to consider," Jesse put in. "If it becomes the main shipping point for cattle going north to Chicago, there's no limit to how big the town can be. Otherwise, it will just stay a small farming community."

Stella spoke up, her voice sharp. "And what, may I ask, is wrong with a small farming community? A lot of people like it just the way it is!"

"I'm afraid there's no way Abilene or any other part of Kansas is going to stay just the way it is," Laramie said. "Texas cattle will be shipped north. If not through Abilene, then through some other town nearby. I'm not saying it's good or that I'm in favor of it, but that's the way it is, and not you nor me nor any town is going to stop it in the long run."

"That's what I've been trying to tell him," Jesse growled. "It will be better for everyone in the long run."

"Oh, be quiet, Jesse!" Forrest said with sudden harshness. He strode to the window and gazed out into the night for a long time, puffing stolidly on his cigar. Finally he turned back. "Of course you're right, Nelson. I know that, deep in my gut. But these people here, they're my friends, they trust me. It's their feeling, mine too, that if the Texas herds come to Abilene, their own stock will get the fever. I must stand with them, my neighbors."

Laramie said dryly, "Is that why you brought in those ex-Rebel roughnecks and renegades?"

Forrest pounded a fist into his open palm. "That wasn't any of my doing! I had hoped we could use other means, but there's a hothead among the farmers who feels that a show of strength is the only way."

"Who might that be?"

"His name is Tom Chaney, and I'm damned if I thought he had the brass to go ahead and get those Quantrill men in here on his own. But they're here and taking their orders from Chaney, not me, and it looks like we're stuck with 'em."

"I reckon I don't have to tell you the Texas drovers aren't going to take it lying down," Laramie said. "They'll be back, and the next time they'll have fire power of their own to match yours."

Forrest sighed. "Yes, I'm afraid there will be some shooting."

"It'll be more than some," Laramie said sharply. "There are some folks already who want to get the Army into this. And I think most of us have seen all we want to of war. Blood will run like water."

Stella walked over to her father's side and touched his arm lightly. "There's something in what Laramie says, Dad. No stand is worth all the killing that may come out of all this."

For a moment the gray-haired man pressed his own hand to his daughter's. Then he turned his face away. "I'm sorry, Stella. I can't go against my neighbors."

Jesse said with a thin sneer, "To my way of thinking, it's a matter of progress, progress and money."

"Jesse, would you leave us alone?" Forrest said harshly.

Jesse flushed bright red, then stalked from the parlor with as much dignity as he could muster.

When Forrest turned again to Laramie, his shoulders were slumped, and he looked suddenly older. "If that boy only had the gumption his sister has."

"Stella seems a fine girl," Laramie said in a neutral voice.

"She's all of that, and more. Sometimes I worry that I'm favoring her over Jesse because she's my own flesh and blood. But it's not true. I've given that boy every possible chance to show that he cares about the land and the stock and especially other people. The only way Jesse seems to measure the worth of anything is in dollars. It's a cruel thing to say, but sometimes I think he's just waiting for me to pass on so he can get the farm here and turn it into dollars!"

Forrest shook his big head as though shedding his personal problems like droplets of water. "Sorry, Nelson. I didn't mean to bang your ear with a lot of family problems. I wish I could help you, because I think you're trying to do the fair thing here. But I told you the reason I can't."

"I appreciate your being honest with me," Laramie said. "Would you do this much—would you get as many of the farmers and ranchers around here together and have them meet me here at your place tomorrow? I'd like to talk to them, feel them out, hear what they have to say. Maybe I can talk them into abandoning the blockade or at least agreeing to some sort of compromise."

"I'll be glad to," Forrest said immediately. "At least I can do that much for you."

"Thank you. Now I'd better be getting back to town."

"Do you think it's safe, with a bushwhacker lurking out there?"

"It's safe enough. The bushwhacker likely won't make two tries in one night.

"I'll have them here for you tomorrow evening, Nelson. Depend on it."

Stanley Forrest stood in the doorway watching Laramie stride toward the barns. Finally he turned back inside the house.

Laramie led the pinto out into the night air, where he cinched up the saddle rig. As he started to mount up, he saw a figure hurrying toward him from the house. He waited, steadying the horse.

It was Stella. She stopped an arm's length away and studied him, the pale October stars reflected like points of light in her eyes. She said, "I didn't want you to get away before I apologized for the way I acted tonight."

"No apology necessary," Laramie said.

"That isn't like me, not really, running out of a room like that. It's just that I'm afraid for Dad. He's being drawn into a fight he really doesn't want because of his sense of loyalty to his friends. Why can't men learn to settle things without fighting and killing? I'm sorry, I must sound like a typical, weepy woman to you."

"Being against killing is nothing to be sorry for. A man would have to be crazy to think otherwise."

"But what about your job, Laramie? There must be times when you have to kill other men."

"There are times," he said laconically.

"How does it make you feel to know you're to blame

for the death of another man?"

"Bad. It makes me feel plain bad, if you really want to know."

Stella touched his arm, and Laramie could feel the warmth of her fingers through the material of his shirt. She said, "You know, I do owe you an apology. I made a snap judgement when I saw you knock that man down in the street. I thought you were no better than a brawler and another gunman. I was wrong, Laramie. There is much more to you than that."

"Don't be too sure," he said. "I've been in more brawls and gunfights than most men, and I don't reckon I'm through with them yet."

"Have you ever thought of quitting? Have you ever seen one place you'd like to stay and, well, one person you'd like to stay with? Have you ever wanted to lead a different kind of life, more like other men?"

"Oh, I've thought about it often enough," he replied. "I've thought about it nights when I've had to sleep on the frozen ground. I've thought about it at Christmas time when I see families together. I think about it every time I look into the eyes of a man I'm about to kill. Yes, Stella, I think about living another kind of life. But it wouldn't work. It's not my style."

"Maybe you'll change your mind one day."

"Maybe I will."

Stella stepped back. "Good night, Laramie. I'll see you at the meeting tomorrow. I hope we can talk them out of the showdown they're h ⁀ding for."

"I sure hope so. Good night, Stella Forrest."

The girl took a step toward him hesitated, then turned and walked toward the distant house without looking back. Laramie watched until the door closed behind her. Somewhere in the night a coyote howled, a lonely and desolate sound.

Laramie mounted up and headed back toward Abilene.

The next morning early Laramie Nelson ate a huge breakfast of steak and eggs. Then he walked up to the train depot, where he pulled a grumbling telegraph operator out of a checker game and had him tap out a message to Brock Peters in Denver. Laramie told the operator he expected an answer later in the day.

A half hour later Laramie was again riding south on the road out of Abilene. This time, however, he bore to the left on a wagon road that branched off the main road about a mile outside of town. A short ride brought him to a fair-sized house of logs caulked with clay. Dirt was banked around the bottom of the structure to keep out the weather.

A scrawny boy of about fourteen trudged toward the house carrying two pails of water from a well about forty yards distant. The boy stopped, setting the pails down, and watched Laramie ride up.

"Howdy, younker," Laramie said. "They told me in town that the Chaney place was out this way."

"This is the Chaney place, mister," the boy said. "You lookin' for my pa?"

"If his name's Tom Chaney, I am."

"He's out in back. I'm Andrew."

"Pleased to meet you, Andrew."

Laramie clucked to the rented horse and rode around to the rear of the log house, where a wiry man with an upstanding brush of black hair hammered at the hub of a wagon wheel, cursing in time to the hammer blows.

Laramie swung down and walked up behind the man. "Tom Chaney?"

The man straightened and turned. He had an angry, scowling face, with prominent cheekbones and a thin, beaked nose. "That's right. And who're you?"

"The name is Laramie Nelson."

"Oh, yeah, the Pinkerton man." Chaney grunted and spat a brown stream of tobacco juice on the ground and scoured at it absently with the toe of his boot. "What do you want with me?"

"They tell me you're the one to blame for bringing in these Quantrill raiders who turned back the herd of longhorns."

"What if I am?"

"Are you also willing to take the blame for the bloodshed that's likely to come?"

"Won't be any bloodshed if them drovers steer clear of Abilene."

"They can't do that, and you know it," Laramie retorted. "They brought their herd this far because the businessmen of Abilene told them they could ship from here. With winter coming on, the drovers can't turn back, and they can't go anywhere else."

"That ain't my lookout," Chaney said stubbornly.

"If the blockade continues, the Texans will fight."

"Let 'em fight. We're ready for them."

"I wonder." Laramie looked at the log house, the battered wagon, the leaning barn with uneven gaps between the rough boards of the walls. "You know, I'm surprised that you make enough off this spread to hire that band of cutthroats. I've never known that kind to work for anything but cash on the barrelhead. How do you pay them, Chaney?"

"That ain't none of your business!"

"You're wrong. It is my business."

"I think you better get off my land, mister."

As Chaney's voice rose, the back door to the house opened, and a pale woman, stooped and worn from years of hard work, emerged and came toward them.

"Is anything wrong, Tom?" she asked apprehensively.

"Nothing's wrong. I was just saying good-by to Mr. Pinkerton here. You get on back inside, Ada."

Laramie swung up into the saddle. He touched the brim of his hat.

"Ma'am," he said to Mrs. Chaney.

The woman nodded to him awkwardly and scurried back into the house.

To Chaney, Laramie said, "There's a meeting tonight at Stanley Forrest's place. Do you know it?"

"I've heard," Chaney said, "and I'll be there. But don't think you're gonna talk me into anything!"

Chaney picked up his hammer and attacked the wheel viciously before Laramie had ridden twenty yards.

IV

Shortly before dark Laramie Nelson had picked up the telegram from Brock Peters. He read it twice, nodded to himself with satisfaction. Peter, with his usual thoroughness, had wired the information Laramie had wanted.

It was full dark when Laramie rode south out of Abilene toward Stanley Forrest's place. A high, pale moon kept pace with him behind a ragged curtain of clouds. A frosty wind snatched at the breath of both horse and rider. This time Laramie took extra care when he reached the cottonwood grove where the ambusher had waited the night before. Tonight nothing stirred in the woods, except the small animals that belonged there.

From the number of rigs and horses in the Forrest yard, it seemed most of Forrest's neighbors must be there already. That was the way Laramie had planned it, so they could get all their private talk out of the way before he said his piece. He didn't have a great deal of hope that he could talk them into lifting the blockade, but he had to make the effort.

A hired man was on the job this time, and took Laramie's horse away. As Laramie mounted the porch steps, Stanley Forrest and Stella came out to meet him.

"Evening, Nelson," Forrest said. "Everybody's inside waiting for you."

Stella slipped her arm through Laramie's with a naturalness that caused her father to cock an eyebrow, then smile to himself.

"Good luck tonight, Laramie," Stella said. "You'll have to be pretty convincing to sway these bullheads. They have already heard everything Harlan Vane and his businessmen's committee have to say."

"I'll do my best," said Laramie, and walked with Stella and her father into the large front room of the Forrest house.

There were some twenty men in the room. Their faces were weathered and aged from exposure to the elements. Their hands were calloused and their muscles hard from years of making a living off the land. Near the back of the room Laramie picked out the scowling face of Tom Chaney. A few feet away stood Jesse Forrest, his smooth, pale features looking very much out of place.

100

Forrest walked to the front of the room and held up his hands for silence. He said, "Men, this here is Laramie Nelson from the Pinkerton Agency. You all know why he's in Abilene, now I'd appreciate it if you'd give him your full attention."

"He's got nothin' we want to hear," Chaney growled.

"Tom, would you be good enough to shut your big mouth until Laramie's had his say?" Forrest said. "Is that too much to ask?"

The other men murmured their agreement and turned to Laramie, their eyes challenging.

Laramie looked over his audience, meeting each man's gaze briefly. He said, "I'm not going to talk to you men about the economic future of Kansas or how the prosperity of Abilene depends on shipping the big Texas trail herds from there. These things are important, but you've heard them before. I'm going to talk to you about ticks, because that's what this is really all about, isn't it?"

The men muttered their assent and crowded closer.

"I know what tick fever can do to your stock," Laramie went on. "I also know that to a man with sick and dying stock, the prosperity of Abilene doesn't mean buffalo chips.

"But there was still a lot I didn't know about ticks, so I sent a wire this morning to my chief in Denver and asked for more information. I have his answer here with me," Laramie tapped his pocket, "if any of you want to read it later. One thing I found out is that there are hundreds of different kinds of mites and ticks, but only two of them can infect the blood of your stock and cause the fever. Knowing Texas longhorns, we can be pretty sure they'll carry a lot of ticks into Abilene. But unless the ticks are one of two kinds, I've got the long Latin names here in

101

case you're interested, they can't do any harm."

"How are we supposed to know what kind of ticks they are?" one of the men asked. "One tick looks just like another to this hoss."

"That's right," Chaney said, elbowing his way forward. "We got too much to lose to take a gamble like that. I say we keep these damned longhorns out of Abilene. That way we'll be sure."

Laramie raised his voice above the growing rumble of agreement. "I'm not asking you to gamble on anything. There's a man in Kansas City from the U. S. Department of Agriculture. If you all agree, he can be here by day after tomorrow to set up an inspection station. Then he'll be able to tell us if any of the longhorns are carrying the kind of ticks that could bring in the fever."

The men gathered in the room turned to each other, and in the tone of their individual conversations Laramie could hear a swelling note of agreement.

"Now just hold on a minute, you people!" Chaney said loudly. "It may be all well and good to have a Government feller tell us whether them longhorns are goin' to bring in the fever or not. But what if he says, yes, they are? Do you think them drovers are goin' to say, sorry, folks, and turn their herd around and head back home? Not on your life, they ain't! We'll have to fight them sooner or later anyhow. I say, let's fight now!"

"Let me answer your question, Chaney," Laramie said quietly. "Some men in North Carolina have come up with a cattle dip that has completely wiped out the fever ticks in the places they have tried it. Someday they'll be using it all over the country, but right now, if it's necessary, every steer in the Texas herds can be treated before they come north of the Cottonwood River. I'll guarantee you the drovers will agree to that."

"What good's your guarantee?" Chaney said with a sneer. "And how do we know that'll work? I ain't never heard of any cattle dip like that. What I say is—"

"We've all heard plenty of what you say, Chaney," Forrest cut in. "Sounds to me like you're plain trying to stir up more trouble than we already have. Nelson's answered all your questions, and what he says makes good sense to me. I think we ought to have a show of hands on it!"

A chorus of, "Yes, yes, let's have a vote," came from the crowd, and Laramie Nelson sensed that it was going his way. From the doorway in the back of the room Stella gave him a warm smile and made a silent applauding motion with her hands.

Forrest motioned for quiet. "All right, all in favor raise your hands—"

The sound of a running horse out front silenced him, and all eyes swung to the door as a rider dismounted outside, clomped across the porch and burst into the room.

"Night riders!" the newcomer said breathlessly.

"What is it, man?" Forrest snapped. "Out with it!"

"Tom Chaney's place. Heard gunfire when I was ridin' past. Six, seven, maybe ten men outside on horseback, firing into the house. Somebody was shootin' back at 'em from inside, but I knowed all you men was over here, so I rode hell for leather!"

"What are we waiting for?" somebody shouted. "Let's go get 'em!"

"My old woman and boy are there alone," Chaney

103

cried. He glared at Laramie. "What good's your cattle dip now, Mr. Pinkerton?"

Chaney dashed for the door, the others in his wake.

For a moment Stanley Forrest stood facing Laramie, face etched in gloom. "I don't know what this means, Nelson, but I'm afraid it's bad trouble."

"We can talk about it later," Laramie said tersely. "Right now Chaney's wife and son need our help immediately."

And he was out of the door and running toward the barns for his horse.

Laramie, and four of the men who had horses, galloped out of Forrest's yard, followed by the rest in two wagonloads. By the time they reached the wagon trail leading to Chaney's place, the sound of gunfire could be clearly heard from the direction of the house.

As they rode within sight of the house, half a dozen or so mounted men could be seen in the pale moonlight, circling the building and firing into it with repeating rifles. An occasional flash and boom answered from a window. As Laramie and the others began firing from a distance, a shout of alarm was heard from the raiders, and they broke off their attack, galloping up over a low rise to the north of the house.

Tom Chaney leaped from his horse and ran toward the house. Before he reached it the door opened, and his wife stepped out. Her body sagged with a weariness beyond words. In her hand, hanging straight down at her side, was an old muzzle-loading Springfield. At the sight of her husband, she dropped the rifle to the ground.

"They shot Andrew," the woman said dully.

Chaney stopped as though struck across the face.

"They killed our boy." Ada Chaney's voice was flat and

toneless. Her husband grunted sharply and strode past her into the log house.

"Come on," a man shouted angrily, "let's ride after the murderin' galoots!"

"Hold it," Laramie said. "We don't have enough men. By the time the wagons get here, it'll be too late. If we ride over that ridge now, we'll be silhouetted with the moon behind our backs. We'll be picked off like a turkey shoot."

There was some grumbling, but common sense prevailed, and they subsided.

"Texas gunmen," one man said. "We'll know where to find them, down in the drover's camp on the Cottonwood."

Sounds of agreement came from the others, then were cut off by a low, almost animal sound from the house. As a group, they walked to the open door and looked in. Chaney sat crosslegged on the dirt floor, cradling his son's head. The boy's body was limp ans still. The front of his homespun shirt was soaked dark with blood. Chaney looked up at the men with unseeing eyes. Soft moaning sounds came from deep in his chest. Behind him stood his wife, her thin hand on his shoulder in meager comfort.

Several of the men went inside to do what they could for Chaney. Laramie moved off a ways, swearing softly to himself. The wagons loaded with men were arriving.

Stanley Forrest approached Laramie. "It doesn't look good now."

"No, it doesn't," Laramie agreed. "Blast those drovers! Why couldn't they have held off another day or two? We could have had this mess settled peaccably."

"What do you suppose they hoped to gain? Did they think they could frighten us into lifting the blockade?"

"If they did, it was a damn fool mistake. These men are

out for vengeance and blood now. I don't know if they can be stopped."

"I'll do what I can," Forrest said. "Not because my heart isn't with them in what they feel and what they want to do, but because I'm afraid it's a fight they can't win. I don't want to see any more of my neighbors hurt."

"I understand your position," Laramie said. "And I appreciate everything you've tried to do. Let's just hope we can—"

"Dad, can't you do something?" It was Jesse Forrest, hurrying up breathlessly. His eyes were wide, and his voice was higher pitched and louder than usual. "The way those men feel now they could ruin everything!"

Stanley Forrest regarded his stepson for a moment, frowning. He seemed about to speak, then changed his mind and turned away. He said, "I'll talk to you later, Nelson," and walked down the slope toward the house.

Jesse lingered behind. He gestured as though in apology for his stepfather. "You did the best you could, Laramie. They were all but won over to our side. Rotten bad luck that this business had to happen tonight."

"Bad luck." Laramie said tartly. "Yeah, I suppose you could say so. Especially for Tom Chaney and his family."

With another of his apologetic shrugs Jesse turned away toward the house.

Laramie walked the other way, up toward the top of the rise over which the night riders had disappeared. Maybe they had left some sign behind, Laramie thought, although finding anything at night was unlikely.

He went cautiously, every sense alert. He froze in mid-step. Something had moved on the crest of the rise. It was nothing more than a low hump, out of line with the curve of the ground. It could be some night animal.

Then the hump shifted an inch or so, and a gleam of reflected moonlight shone for an instant off the barrel of a rifle.

There was no time to consider courses of action. In a heartbeat Laramie's Colt was in his hand, the barrel laid across his left arm to steady his aim. The rifleman was crouched some seventy-five yards up the slope, about the limit of the Colt's effective range. Laramie squeezed the trigger slowly, and his weapon thundered at almost the same instant as the rifle cracked, spouting a tongue of flame.

There was an outcry from the direction of the Chaney house. And up on the ridge the shadowy hump became a man. He reared up, stumbled once, then vanished over the far side. Laramie started for the spot at a dead run, but before he had covered half the distance the drum of hoofbeats told him that the sniper had made good his escape. Turning back to the house, he saw Stanley Forrest sprawled on the ground. The men stood around him, yammering excitedly.

By the time he reached the house, Laramie found Forrest sitting up, gripping his left arm between the shoulder and elbow and cursing in a monotone. Blood stained the fingers of his right hand.

With the help of one of the others Laramie got Forrest to his feet and opened his coat and shirt, pulling the sleeve away from the injured arm. An angry red furrow creased the flesh. Blood welled out slowly.

"Did you get the dirty backshooters?" Forrest asked. "I heard you fire."

"There was only one, and I'm not sure. If I did, I only winged him. It certainly wasn't bad enough to keep him from riding away."

"Anyway, you spoiled his aim. A couple of inches to the right and I'd be a dead man now."

"It doesn't look too bad. Get it washed and a clean bandage on it as soon as you can."

"I will. What do you suppose they were trying to do, Nelson, leaving one man behind like that?"

"I don't think there's any doubt, he was left there to kill you. He was hiding up there, just waiting to get a good shot. When he got you framed in the lighted doorway, he let fly."

"And so did you, I'm happy to say."

Laramie shrugged. "Mostly luck. I just happened to be looking in the right direction at the right time."

Jesse hurried up. "The wagon's ready to go," he said nervously. "You'd better get home and get that arm attended to."

"I've got something to say to the men first," Forrest said. He stepped away from the man who had been supporting him and stood painfully erect in the doorway to the Chaney house. The others gathered around.

"Men," Forrest began, "this has been a terrible night for all of us. The home of one of our neighbors has been attacked, and his son killed. I know how you feel. You want to hit back. And I'd be a liar if I told you I didn't feel the same way. But I'm asking you to do nothing more tonight."

The men began to grumble.

"Wait a minute now!" Forrest went on. "I don't say back off. But if we act now in hot blood, there could be a lot more of us dead by tomorrow. Go to your homes now. Think it over. Tomorrow we'll decide what's to be done."

With some reluctance they started to disperse. Two of them volunteered to stay with the Chaneys until morning.

The rest found their horses and the wagons and began to leave.

Laramie said good night to Forrest and took a last look into the Chaney house. Tom Chaney sat in a chair now, staring blindly at the wall without moving. Mrs. Chaney had a coffee pot going on the wood stove, while the two men staying stood around uncomfortably.

With the sorrow of the Chaney family a weight across his shoulders, Laramie swung up onto his own horse and headed back for Abilene. The ride to town that night was an unhappy one.

V

There was light in the east by the time Laramie Nelson fell across his narrow bed in the hotel. The thought that he had failed in his assignment to head off bloodshed hammered at him like a fist. Still, there was something about the whole thing that rang false, like an off-tuned piano key. The answer, it seemed, dangled just beyond his reach, and before he could grasp it, he fell into a fitful sleep.

A banging on his door roused him with a start some four hours later. "Who is it?"

"Harlan Vane. Let me in, Nelson."

"Just a minute."

Laramie threw back the covers and swung his legs out of bed. He stepped into his trousers and padded to the floor. Harlan Vane's smooth face was pinker than usual, and he quivered with suppressed anger. Laramie walked away to splash cold water on his face, and let Vane follow him in.

"I heard about what happened out at the Chaney place

last night," Vane said.

"That so?"

"The whole town has heard about it. Now I want some kind of an explanation from you, Nelson!"

Laramie toweled his face dry and hung up the towel. He crossed to the chair where he had draped his shirt the night before, took a sack of Bull Durham and papers from the pocket, and rolled a cigarette. He said mildly, "Just what is it you wanted explained, Mr. Vane?"

Vane waved his arms. "How could you let a thing like this happen?"

"I don't see how I could have stopped it."

"You might have worked with me and the committee when you first got here instead of charging off on your own!"

"I was doing just fine by myself until those night riders showed up."

"You can't blame the cattlemen too much for that," Vane said. "They certainly had provocation."

Laramie turned a flat stare on the man. "Provocation to shoot down a fourteen-year-old boy?"

"They couldn't have known who was in the house," Vane said, flushing slightly.

"I wonder."

"Anyway, one of them was killed, too, so now I suppose both sides will be out for blood. Are you ready to—?"

"Wait a minute! You say one of the night riders was killed?"

"That's right. Couple of youngsters out hunting jack rabbits found this horse wandering free and backtracked until they found a man dead with a bullet in his chest."

110

Laramie grabbed his shirt and began pulling it on in a hurry. "Know who it is?"

"I haven't seen the body."

"Where is it, the body?"

"In the barber shop down the street."

"The barber shop?" Laramie repeated.

"In the back room. Our barber is also the undertaker. Why?"

Laramie was buckling on his gunbelt. "I don't know exactly. It's just a hunch I have that I should take a look."

"But what about the committee? They want a report," Vane said. "What will I tell them?"

"Tell them to draw up a resolution about something."

Laramie pushed past the spluttering Vane and strode down the hall to the stairs.

The hotel desk clerk told him that the barber shop was down the street from the Bull's Head. As he walked quickly down the dusty street, Laramie slowly became aware of something different about Abilene this morning. Something was missing. Suddenly he knew what it was. The Quantrill men were gone! That could mean more grief. If the ex-guerrillas were not here in Abilene, that meant trouble was likely building somewhere.

The barber shop had a plank nailed beside the door, a plank with crude red and white diagonal stripes to advertise the business. Inside, the one barber chair was empty.

Laramie walked past it to a soiled green curtain that hung across the width of the room. He pushed the curtain aside and stepped into the back part of the building. A body covered with a stained sheet lay on a wooden table in the center of the room. At a counter along the far wall a white-coated man with shiny black hair and a pencil mustache was writing something in a ledger. He glanced up and smiled at Laramie, showing small, regular teeth.

"Barber shop closed until noon," he said cheerfully. "Guess I forgot to put up the sign."

"I'm not here for barbering," Laramie said. "I'd like a look at your customer."

"Kin of the deceased?"

"Not exactly. I'm with the Pinkertons."

Laramie pulled out his impressive-looking credentials and showed them to the barber-undertaker. Though the credentials gave him little official standing, Laramie had found out long ago they often saved a lot of unnecessary conversation.

"Sure thing, Mr. Nelson. Let me fold the sheet back." Deftly, the undertaker exposed the upper half of the body on the table. "Bullet caught him in the right lung. I figure he rode some two miles before he bled to death."

"Has anybody else been asking about him?"

"Nope. You're the only one."

Laramie stood gazing down at the dead man. The whiskey flush had drained away with the blood, but Laramie recognized the beefy, broken-nosed face as that of the man who had challenged him in the street his first day in Abilene.

"What did he have in his pockets?"

"Nothing much. Matches, couple of cheap stogies— Oh, and a twenty-dollar gold piece. Don't know where a fella like him could ever come up with that."

"Thanks," Laramie said slowly, "you've been a help."

"Glad to do it. Come back this afternoon, I'll give you as close a shave as you ever had."

"Some other time," Laramie said, and walked through

112

the green curtain and out into the street.

Many questions raced through his mind. Why would one of the Quantrill men be among the night riders shooting up the house of Tom Chaney, the very man who was supposed to be paying them? And what was his reason for trying to kill Stanley Forrest? Could the double eagle in his picket have been a payment for Forrest's life? These questions chased each other through Laramie's mind as he walked back toward the hotel. In mid-stride he changed direction and headed toward the livery stable. It wasn't a meeting he was looking forward to, but the place to get some answers was from Tom Chaney.

Nothing moved at the Chaney place except dry leaves the wind sent skittering along the ground. No smoke rose from the chimney, even though the wind had a chill bite. Laramie reined up before the house and tied his horse to the rail. He knocked on the door and waited. When there was no response, he knocked again. This time someone moved inside, and slow footsteps approached across the floor.

Ada Chaney opened the door and peered out. "What do you want?"

"Is you husband here, Mrs. Chaney?"

"No."

"Can you tell me where he is?"

"Why should I?"

"It's very important," Laramie said. "I wouldn't bother you otherwise."

"Nothing's important any more," she said listlessly. "Our boy is dead, and there's no reason to go on."

"I'm real sorry about your boy, Mrs. Chaney. If I can talk to Tom Chaney, maybe we can stop more killing."

"Tom says you're to blame for Andrew bein' dead."

"That's not fair, Mrs. Chaney."

"Maybe it ain't, but that's what Tom says. He says if you hadn't come to town and got Stanley Forrest to call that meeting last night Andrew would still be with us."

"You don't believe that, do you, Mrs. Forrest?"

"I stand with my old man."

Since it seemed clear nothing more could be gained there, Laramie touched the brim of his hat and turned to go.

"Wait a minute," the woman said. "He went into town this morning on the lookout for you. He took the rifle. When I saw you at the door I was afraid you'd come to tell me he was dead. The way he was feeling, he might do anything. Look out for him, Mr. Nelson."

"I will, Mrs. Chaney," Laramie said. "And thank you."

Laramie pushed his horse hard on the ride back to Abilene. He took the steps to the broadwalk in front of the hotel in a bound and burst through the door and up to the desk where the clerk was sorting mail.

"Has anybody been here looking for me?"

"There was Mr. Vane this morning. I believe you saw him."

"Anybody else?"

"Uh—one of the nestors from south of town came in a little while ago. Chaney, I believe his name is. Looked like he'd been drinkin' pretty heavy for this time of day."

"What did he say?"

"Nothing. He asked for you. I told him you weren't here and he stomped out. Didn't say where he was going, but I had the feeling he was on his way to slop down some more whiskey."

Laramie thanked the man and walked back out into the street. Again he noticed the strange absence of the

114

Quantrill men, who had seemed to be thick as horse flies when he arrived. As he approached the Bull's Head Saloon, Laramie had the uneasy feeling that unseen eyes were watching him from behind curtained windows.

Before he reached the saloon, the batwing doors swung outward, and Tom Chaney bulled through. He held the old Springfield to his shoulder ready to fire, muzzle pointed directly at Laramie, like a deadly accusing finger.

"Don't come any closer, Pinkerton man," Chaney said. His speech was slurred by liquor, but the rifle was held steady as an oak limb.

Laramie skidded to a stop, arms well extended out from his sides. "Put down the rifle, Chaney. I want a word with you."

"You've done too much talkin' already. While you talked last night, them Texas gunmen was shooting down my boy!"

"Listen to me, Chaney," Laramie said, keeping his voice level and calm. "One of the raiders who attacked your house was shot. They found his body and brought it in this morning."

"What of it? That damned well don't bring my boy back!"

"That man was no Texas gunman, Chaney. He was one of yours, one of the men they say you hired."

"You're a liar!"

"Go look for yourself. He's down at the undertaker's right now."

For several of the longest seconds of Laramie's life, Chaney peered at him unblinkingly down the barrel of the rifle. Laramie knew that the least wrong move could send a bullet crashing into his chest. He held himself tense, hoping that his words had somehow gotten through the man's whiskey-numbed brain.

As they stood motionless, facing each other across the dusty street, Laramie caught a flicker of movement to one side out of the corner of his eyes. Before he could react, a shot rang out. Chaney spun completely around, falling heavily to the wooded sidewalk. The rifle flew out of his hands and landed a few feet away in the street.

Laramie ran to the side of the fallen man and knelt there. Gently, he raised Chaney's head. For a moment Chaney's agonized gaze met Laramie's accusingly. Then all awareness faded from his eyes, and he went limp.

At the sound of running feet Laramie jumped up and spun in a crouch, hand hovering near his gun. It was Jesse Forrest. In his hand was a revolver, smoke spiraling lazily up from the muzzle.

"Whew! That was a close call!" Jesse exclaimed. "I was afraid he'd fire before I could get close enough for a shot."

Laramie gestured angrily at the pistol in Jesse's hand. "What the devil did you do that for?"

Jesse stepped back and blinked several times. "What do you mean?"

"What did you shoot him for?"

"Are you crazy? He was going to kill you. I saved your life, Laramie!"

"Chaney wasn't going to kill anybody," Laramie growled. "He was full of whiskey and grief and wanted to yell at somebody a little, that's all. Men who do a lot of gabbing beforehand don't aim to kill. In another few seconds he would have put the rifle down and it would have been all over."

"You don't know that. And I certainly don't see how I was supposed to know it. I walked out of the store up there and saw Chaney holding a rifle on you. For all I

116

could tell he was all set to blow your head off. I fired to save you. I didn't mean to kill Tom, but I didn't have time to take good aim."

Laramie sighed softly. "I reckon you thought you were doing the right thing, Jesse. There's just so damned many things going wrong! Guess I shouldn't have jumped you like that."

Jesse was only slightly mollified. "You're darn right you shouldn't have. I was only trying to save your hide."

Laramie gazed sadly down at the body. "If I'd just been able to talk to him, a lot of things might have been cleared up."

"Talk to him about what?"

"I shot one of the raiders last night, the one who winged your stepfather. He was able to ride away all right, but his body was found this morning and brought in. I had a look at him. It was the man I had the run-in with the day I got to Abilene."

"One of the very men manning the blockade against the cattle drives?" Jesse was incredulous.

"That's right."

"Why, he must have gone to the cattlemen's camp and sold out!" Jesse said. "Then he came back with that band of gunmen and attacked the house of the man who had hired him in the first place!"

"It looks that way," Laramie admitted.

"How else could it be?"

"Could be he wasn't working for Chaney at all. It had to take a good piece of money to bring him and the rest of these guerrillas in here. Chaney didn't strike me as having that kind of money. It's my guess he was fronting for somebody else."

"Do you know who?" Jesse asked.

117

"No, I don't," Laramie admitted with a shake of his head. "If I knew that, I would have the answers to other bothersome questions, like why was he paid twenty dollars in gold to kill your stepfather?"

"Was he?"

"It sure looks that way."

Tom Chaney's body was taken away, and witnesses were found willing to swear that Jesse had shot Chaney to save Laramie's life. Jesse left in the buckboard for the Forrest spread, and Laramie trudged dejectedly up to his hotel room.

He slammed the door behind him and hurled his Stetson clear across the room and against the far wall. He swore aloud. Two men and a boy were dead so far, with more likely to follow. And he was no closer to heading off trouble, or even getting to the root of it, than when he had stepped off the train. What kind of a report could he possibly make to Brock Peters? What could he say to Joseph McCoy? Some might think it an impossible task for one man to avert a showdown involving a hundred angry men. Typically this did not occur to Laramie. And when Brock Peters sent a Pinkerton man in to do a job, he expected results, no matter how tough the odds.

Laramie's thoughts were interrupted by a tapping on the door. He opened it with a vicious yank, scowling blackly, and Stella Forrest took a startled backward step.

"I'm sorry, Stella," he said, smiling with an effort. "I didn't mean to frighten you. I have other things on my mind. Come in."

"That's all right, Laramie. I met Jesse coming in. He told me what happened. You mustn't blame yourself," she said.

"That's easy enough to say, and I thank you, but it

seems everything I've tried to do on this assignment has turned out sour. What brings you into town?"

Stella was dressed for riding in a long brown skirt trimmed with yellow. Her dark eyes were troubled. "All the men are gathering at our place, Laramie. The Quantrill men are there, too. They're all armed, and they're planning an all-out attack on the cattle camps."

"That's bad news, Stella, but I don't see much I can do about it."

"You could talk to them! They listened to you once."

"Yeah, and while they were listening one of their homes was attacked. I don't think they will be much of a mind to listen to me again soon."

"Laramie, you're the only one who might be able to stop this madness before it gets out of hand. You've got to at least try! Please!"

Laramie retrieved his hat from across the room. "I'll do what I can," he said glumly. "Just don't expect too much."

"All I ask is that you try," Stella said. "Everyone else seems resigned to the fact that there has to be a fight. Even Jesse and Dad."

They walked down the stairs together and into the street in front of the hotel.

"That's my horse over there," Stella said, indicating a little brown mare watching them placidly from the hitching rail.

"How come you're not riding the big bay I saw out there?" Laramie asked.

"Tempest?" the girl said. "That's Jesse's horse. He won't let anybody else near him." She broke off to stare at him. "Laramie, what's the matter?"

For a moment the planes of Laramie's lean face had hardened into a grim mask. Now his expression relaxed somewhat as he gazed down at Stella.

"I think some loose pieces just fell into place," he said. "You go back to your father's place and do what you can to keep the men there. I'll be along in a short while. There's something I have to check out first."

Laramie gave the girl a leg up onto the side-saddled mare, which she sat with the grace of an experienced rider. "All right, Laramie, but come as soon as you can."

"I will, I promise," he said, and watched her ride down the street and make the turn at the far end onto the road leading out of town.

VI

The mood was an ugly one at the Forrest place when Laramie Nelson rode up. On one side of the yard was the ragtag band of Quantrill men. Many of them tilted whiskey bottles, and their loud talk was punctuated by shouts of a coarse laughter and obscenities. On the other side were the Kansas land owners, grim and silent. Both groups were heavily armed.

A mutter went through the crowd as Laramie reined in. One voice rose loud and clear: "It's his fault Tom's boy is dead. And just this morning he was to blame for poor Tom being shot down. Don't listen to nothing he has to say!"

Laramie dismounted at the porch steps where Stanley Forrest stood with his daughter and stepson.

"It's no good, Nelson," Forrest said. "The men are determined to fight it out now with the cattlemen from Texas. Nothing I can say will stop them."

"I've learned some things that might change their minds," Laramie said.

"We want no more of your slick gab, Pinkerton man!" a voice called from the crowd.

"Go on back where you came from!"

"This is our fight now, we don't need you!"

"Let's run him out of the territory!"

"I'm sorry, Nelson," Forrest said, "but you see how it is. I think you'd better leave."

Most of them were shouting derisively at Laramie now, urged on by the ex-guerrillas, who had moved in closer behind the others.

With deadly speed Laramie whipped around, drawing his Colt. He fired three times over their heads. The sudden burst of gunfire was enough to stun the men into silence.

Laramie holstered his gun and drawled, "Now you men listen to me before you run off in all directions and do something you'll be sorry for all your lives. You think you're going to ride down and get even with the men who shot down Chaney's boy, do you? Well, you're wrong! All you'll find in that Cottonwood River camp is a bunch of innocent cowmen who only want one thing, to get their herd to market. The men who rode in the night to attack a woman and a boy came from that gang of saddle tramps behind you, the scum you think is fighting on your side!"

"Now hold on, Nelson!" Forrest said. "If you're saying that because the man who took a shot at me was one of them, Jesse has already told us about that. You can't blame the whole bunch just because one of them sold out and turned renagade."

"That's Jesse's theory," Laramie retorted. "It doesn't happen to be mine."

Jesse Forrest spoke up then, standing to one side and slightly to the rear of his stepfather. "For my part, I'm sick and tired of your theories, Nelson. If you haven't any

121

proof, maybe you'd better ride out of here while you still can."

"You'll hear more proof than you want before I'm finished," Laramie said. He turned to the others, who were listening closely now. Even the ex-guerrillas were quiet and watchful.

Laramie motioned to them. "The word that went around was that these men were brought in here by Chaney. Didn't any of you ever wonder how he could pay them off?"

"We're wasting time," Jesse said loudly. "All he's trying to do is—"

"Let him talk, Jesse," Stanley Forrest said.

Laramie went on, "The man who shot Mr. Forrest here, and was killed in the doing, had a twenty-dollar gold piece on him when he was found. I don't think it would have been easy for Chaney to come up with even that much. How many of the rest of you could?"

"Money ain't easy to come by these hard times," said a man in the front. He raised his voice. "Are you saying somebody else hired these Quantrill men?"

"That's exactly what I'm saying. Chaney was acting as a front."

"Then this somebody else ordered them to shoot up Tom's place, and paid one of them extra to kill Mr. Forrest?"

"That's the way it shapes up," Laramie said.

Stanley Forrest faced Laramie squarely. "You're making a very serious accusation, Nelson. I'd like to hear who you're accusing of all this."

Before Laramie could reply a horse and wagon rattled into the yard. A lone woman rode the wagon seat.

122

"Here's someone who can tell you better than I can," Laramie said.

He strode across the yard and helped Ada Chaney down from the wagon. The men parted before them to make a path as Laramie led the woman to the porch steps.

Laramie said, "I asked Mrs. Chaney to come here because you're not going to like what has to be said, and I figured you'll be more ready to hear it from her than you would from me." He turned to the woman. "Mrs. Chaney, did your husband bring these Quantrill men in here to blockade the Texas herds?"

The woman's voice was low, despairing, but it carried clearly in the crisp autumn air. "Tom wouldn't have known how to do anything like that on his own. He was a farmer. 'Sides, how could he pay them?"

"So somebody talked him into pretending that it was his doing?"

"That's right, Mister. He gave Tom the money to pay these men, and he gave the orders for Tom to pass along. Tom thought he was doin' the right thing for everybody concerned."

"Did your husband know anything about the plan to kill Mr. Forrest?"

"Oh, no! My Tom had a right mean temper on him sometimes, but he never wanted nobody killed. Especially Mr. Forrest. Tom respected Mr. Forrest."

"Tell us, please, Mrs. Chaney, who was the man your husband was acting for?"

Ada Chaney stood erect and leveled a trembling finger. "Him there. Jesse Forrest!"

For a long moment the only sound heard was the sighing of the Kansas wind. Then there was a general

123

shuffling as the men turned as one to stare at Jesse.

Jesse laughed shakily. "She's crazy! She's only saying that because I had to shoot her husband this morning!"

"No, you're the one, Jesse," the widow said steadily. "You came to the house and gave Tom money and told him what to do. My Tom told me, and he never lied. Then you killed him."

"That's a barefaced lie! I only shot Tom to save this—this Pinkerton's life."

"No, Jesse, that isn't why you killed Chaney," Laramie said. "You overheard me tell him that at least one of the men who raided his house was a member of the Quantrill bunch. Given time to think that over, he would have realized he was being used. So you silenced him before he could talk."

Jesse spread his hands and appealed to those listening. "Now why would I do all these things? You all know that I was opposed to the blockade. I was against all of you in that. I wanted the cattle to get through."

"You didn't care one way or the other about the cattle," Laramie said. "You took that stand to throw suspicion off yourself. What you stood to gain was your stepfather's ranch, one of the richest spreads in the state. You hoped your stepfather would lead the battle against the cattlemen and get killed in the doing. Then the ranch would be yours."

"Why would I go to all the trouble just to kill one man?" Jesse sneered. "I could have hired any gunman to do that!"

"Yes, you could," Laramie said. "But the way I figure it, this place wasn't enough for you. You're greedy. In all the bloodshed, there would be a lot of smaller places around here suddenly up for sale for a song. You'd be able

124

to control most of the land south of Abilene all the way to the Cottonwood River."

Stanley Forrest, who had listened silently all the while, now stirred restlessly. "If you know Jesse was behind all this, why wait until now to tell us?"

"Trouble is, I didn't know myself until today," Laramie confessed somewhat sheepishly. "Stella told me, in a way."

"Me?" Stella's hand fluttered to her throat. "But I had no idea—"

"It was your horse, actually. You know the first night I rode out here? Somebody tried to bushwhack me, remember? When I got here, I walked out with Jesse to stable my horse. There was a big bay gelding in the bar, still damp, a blanket over him. I knew he'd just been ridden, but I didn't think much of it at the time. Jesse told me it was Stella's horse, but I found out today, when I saw Stella's little mare, that he had lied. He was afraid I might connect up between his horse being just back from being ridden hard and the bushwhacker galloping away after missing me."

"Laramie," Stella said in distress, "you mean it was Jesse who tried to kill you that night?"

"I'm afraid so, Stella," Laramie said, facing her. "I suppose he was afraid I might ruin his plans."

Looking away from Jesse almost cost Laramie his life. He caught a flicker of movement on the edge of his vision. He threw himself down and to the right just as Jesse's gun blasted, the bullet whistling inches past Laramie's cheek.

Laramie's leap carried him off the porch. He hit the hard ground rolling, the impact driving the breath from his lungs. He rolled over twice, clawing for his gun. He heard Jesse's gun boom again.

Then Laramie came up on his left elbow. He snapped off one shot, knew he had missed, and took a moment to steady himself for the second.

This time his aim was true. His bullet struck Jesse Forrest in the heart. Jesse went flying backward under the impact, his own gun going off once more, the bullet plowing into the ground close to Laramie. Jesse stumbled off the porch and fell to the ground on his back and was still.

For a long moment the acrid stench of gunpowder hung over the scene. Then the brisk wind blew the smoke away, and everyone seemed to move at once. Stanley Forrest was the first to reach his stepson's side. He kneeled beside him.

Laramie got to his feet and approached the fallen man.

From his kneeling position Stanley Forrest looked up. He said in a dead voice, "He's gone. Jesse is dead."

"I'm sorry, Mr. Forrest," Laramie said gently.

"Jesse drew first," one of the men said. "There was nothin' else the Pinkerton man could do, Stanley."

"I know that, I saw it all." Forrest got stiffly to his feet. "I'm not blaming you, Nelson. You had to do it. Jesse wasn't much, and he did a lot of things it looks like I'll be a long time payin' for. But he was the closest thing I had to a son." He passed a hand over his eyes. "I'd appreciate it if you'd all leave me alone with my dead."

Stella, eyes flooded with tears, stood by her father's side. She didn't look at Laramie.

Laramie took a step toward her, then changed his mind and veered away.

He had noticed the Quantrill raiders edging toward their horses even before the shooting started. Now they were nearly all gone.

The farmers and ranchers watched them go with hard eyes. It was not likely, Laramie thought, that such a band of cutthroats would soon be seen in this part of Kansas again.

Now the others were moving toward the horses and wagons. A few paused for a brief word of commiseration with Sanley Forrest. Soon the yard was empty for the Forrests and Laramie.

It was all over.

As Laramie untied his rented horse, he felt a light touch on his arm. He turned to look into Stella's dark eyes, still wet with tears she made no effort to hide.

"You were leaving without saying good-bye?" she said reproachfully.

"I didn't think you—" Laramie cleared his throat. "I did kill your stepbrother."

Stella turned her face away briefly, then squared her shoulders resolutely and looked at him again. "I'm sorry things had to end this way, Laramie."

"So am I, Stella, so am I."

"But this is your way of life, isn't it? I don't suppose you'll ever be riding back this way?"

It was in his thoughts to ask if this was an invitation of sorts. But he checked himself, and instead said, "It isn't very likely, Stella. Not unless maybe I'm needed here on another job."

Stella opened her lips to speak again, but her voice broke on a sob. "Good-by then, Laramie," she whispered, and hurried to join her father, who stood with bowed head over the body of his stepson.

Laramie watched them for a moment, then mounted up. As he swung the horse around, Mrs. Forrest came running out of the house, skirt billowing in the wind.

127

Laramie started his horse off at a trot. Before he was out of hearing, a piercing scream of grief came from Mrs. Forrest. Laramie dug his heels into the horse's flank and sent him toward Abilene at a gallop.

A few days later, Laramie Nelson stood on a raised platform watching the scene before him.

The air swirled with choking dust and straw, and the smell of cattle was strong as whooping cowboys herded the longhorns into the new Abilene stockyards at the Kansas Pacific siding. The cattle bawled and milled angrily, tossing horns reflecting the bright sunlight. Occasionally one broke free and tried to escape, a cowpuncher spurring in pursuit.

The pens slowly filled beside Nelson, natty in a beaver-trimmed coat, stood a beaming Joseph McCoy.

McCoy placed a hand on Laramie's shoulder.

"Thirty-five hundred head," he said. "And this is only the beginning. You're seeing history being made, Nelson. In the next few years Abilene is going to see a trail-driving boom the like of which the West has never known and likely will never know again. You can be real proud of the part you played in opening up Abilene to the big Texas trail herds."

"Yeah," Laramie said dryly. Then he moved his shoulders, impatient with himself. "I'm glad it worked out. And I'm glad my job is done."

McCoy looked at him with quick understanding. "I heard there were some unpleasant moments. I'm sorry, Nelson."

"There always are. It goes with the job."

"Yes, I daresay." For a thoughtful moment, McCoy studied the younger man. "Tell me, Nelson, do you ever think of leaving the Pinkertons? Maybe it's none of my business, but I can't help wondering if a man like you ever thinks about settling down somewhere with a wife and raising a family in some kind of work where you wouldn't always have to worry about getting shot at."

Laramie's gray eyes scanned the flat land stretching south from Abilene, as though an answer might be there. Then he looked levelly at his companion. "No, Mr. McCoy, I never think about it."

"Well, if you ever do, come see me," McCoy said heartily. "I can always use a man like you in my business."

The hooting of a train whistle filled the momentary gap in their conversation. Laramie glanced down the tracks at the train approaching about a half mile away.

"There's my train," he said. He shook the other man's hand and picked up his bag from the platform. "Good-by, Mr. McCoy, and good luck with the trail herds."

"The same to you, my friend," McCoy said.

Laramie Nelson stepped down from the platform and walked toward the train depot without once looking back, dust from the cattle pens billowing around him like brown smoke.

GUN MISSION FOR THE PRESIDENT

I

Had there not been an observer, the wagon train's fate might have remained a mystery for all time. The fact that there was a stray packsaddle miner wandering the ridges above the Nevada desert was unfortunate for the ambushers, but it provided the nation with exciting news—news that could only be partly suppressed.

A Federal Government wagon train had been overwhelmed, a dozen men killed, several horses and mules destroyed along with ten wagons, and five wagons had disappeared. At the time the telegraph message went out, the missing wagons had not been found.

"They run off to the south," the miner reported. "They was mebbe thirty of 'em, riding like billy-be-damned when they hit that wagon train. First thing you know they was shootin' and yellin'. Reminded me of a Redskin raid. And then all of a sudden it was all over."

"You mean the defenders didn't even put up a fight?" he was asked.

"They didn't have no time," the miner said. "They was hit jest right, in between two hills. Them bushwhackers came at 'em from front and back and it war all over in a minute or two."

"Then what happened?"

"Why, they jest run the rest of them fellers off, shootin' in the air. Then they loaded everything in five wagons. They sure took a hour at it, and headed south with them."

The newspaper reports of the ambush were vague, even with the miner's tale. A government spokesman quickly held a press conference, explaining that the outlaws had raided the train for weapons and had escaped with a dozen cases of arms and ammunition, which was what the miner witnessed being transferred from the destroyed wagons to the five driven away.

The five missing wagons were found two days later, a dozen miles from the scene of the ambush. They had been burned down to the rims. According to official reports, experienced trackers were presently at work, attempting to bring the outlaws to justice.

That was the story as Laramie Nelson read it in the Washington *Tribune*, while waiting for Brock Peters in the lobby of the Bakeland Hotel in Washington City.

Laramie was uncomfortable in a gray suit, a tie and laced shoes. He had spent equally uncomfortable days on the train from Denver to Chicago, then to Baltimore and Washington City at Brock Peters' urgent request. Something was up certainly, but he knew it was useless to conjecture until he had the full story from Brock Peters, his Pinkerton superior. He knew it had to be big for Peters to send him kiting all the way across the country.

Laramie sighed, leaned back and rolled a cigarette. He

134

was tall, slender, with a lean face that rarely smiled. His gray eyes, slightly squinted from years spent under the scalding plains sun, made him seem even more out of place.

He had just finished the cigarette when Brock Peters came bustling into the hotel lobby.

Peters didn't look at all out of place. But then he always wore Eastern clothes, even in Denver and other points west. Strangely enough, he didn't look out of place there, either. He was a small man, with a round face. The innocent look he habitually wore was deceptive. He could handle himself well in any environment, as he had proved repeatedly to Laramie.

Although Laramie hadn't seen the man in months, Peters didn't waste time on the amenities. He hustled Laramie Nelson into the hotel dining room, ordered dinner, then asked Laramie if he'd heard about the wagon train.

Laramie admitted that he had.

"You know that country, do you?"

Laramie shrugged. "I've ridden over it, but it's not my home range."

Peters grinned impishly. "I've already told the President you know it well."

"The President! You're joshing me!"

Peters leaned close. His gaze darted about the huge dining room before he spoke. "You're to say nothing, mind. This is secret as a thing can get. But I want you to be thinking about that country because that's where you're heading, come tomorrow."

"I leave here tomorrow?"

"Right after you see the President."

Laramie drew a deep breath. Peters had a way of hitting him in the bread basket with both feet. In fact, he seemed to take great delight in it, as Laramie had learned in the past.

Laramie spent a restless night. The very thought of an audience with President Ulysses S. Grant made him extremely nervous.

The next morning they cooled their heels for two hours in the waiting room before being called in for their appointment. They read a dozen newspapers, smoked too much, talked, paced and stared at the clerks and solemn-faced officials who seemed to come and go like the tides back and forth in the hallways.

"You're sure we're supposed to be here?" Laramie asked several times, and each time Peters only growled. But eventually they were escorted into the President's office.

President Grant was shorter than Laramie had thought he would be, a tough-looking, grizzled man with an indoor pallor, a cigar fuming in his beard. Laramie Nelson shook hands, trying not to stare. In civilian clothes President Grant didn't look at all like the mighty warrior who had defeated the battle-wise hosts of Robert E. Lee.

There were three other men present. Two were taller than the President. The third was a bespectacled clerk, who found a chair, produced a notebook and prepared to write.

President Grant said, "This is Mr. George Boutwell, Secretary of the Treasury, and this is my personal aide, Mr. Edward Gans."

"A pleasure," Peters said, shaking hands.

Laramie Nelson merely nodded, shaking hands quickly. The President sat down and fiddled with his cigar.

Gans took the stage. He was slim, wiry, not at all soft-appearing. He had a quick, decisive manner of speaking.

"This is a call for help, gentlemen."

"What about soldiers?" Brock Peters asked.

Gans said, "We've sent soldiers. But we have reason to believe there's more to it than just robbery. That's why we're turning to a private agency like the Pinkertons. You people have done good work for us in the past."

President Grant cleared his throat, spoke through cigar smoke. "There are political undertones, Mr. Peters. We've got to find out who and what's behind it. Troops can guard the gold shipments, but when the soldiers leave the problem will remain."

"The answer isn't guards," Gans said slowly. "It's knowledge, intelligence, finding out who's behind it." He smiled thinly. "That brings us to you, Mr. Nelson."

Laramie was thinking hard. He felt there was more here than he was being told, something they could only hint at without bringing it out into the open. They were all staring at him, even the President, and Laramie knew they were expecting some response. He could think of none and merely nodded.

He shot a measuring glance at Laramie Nelson. "As you no doubt know, the country is in poor financial condition—the war and all."

Gans batted the air with his hand. "But I don't have to tell you about that. The country will prosper, of course, and grow. That's a matter of time. Our needs, however, are more immediate. We need gold now." He locked his

137

hands together behind his back and frowned. "We're scrambling to get back on our feet."

Boutwell said, "The reconstruction of the South is still a drain on the treasury."

Gans swung around. "Yes, yes, that's true, among other things." He stared at Laramie again. "We badly need the gold coming out of Nevada."

So the wagon train was carrying gold, not guns, Laramie thought. He stirred, for a moment afraid he had spoken aloud.

But Gans was going on, "There have been two shipments stolen, an enormous loss to the country. We fear others. It has to stop."

Gans was going on, speaking obliquely of past successes, of confidence and of secrecy, but it was all leading up to the main question. Laramie felt a sense of relief when it finally came. "Will you go to Nevada for us, Mr. Nelson?"

They already knew the answer, of course, but it was nice to be asked. Laramie found himself standing, shaking hands.

For just a moment Laramie was isolated from the others, alone with President Grant. The President, eyes penetrating, said in a low voice, "You'll be on your own on this mission. Mr. Nelson. The need for secrecy is paramount. But it's important to me, to the country."

Then Laramie, feeling slightly dazed, was being ushered out. It struck him that it had been business-like and efficient. He wondered briefly where the newspapers got their ideas about "bumbling" in the White House.

Outside, Peters interrupted his thoughts. "How soon can you catch the train?"

Laramie sighed. It was back to work, out of fancy clothes.

"I'll pack my bag," he said.

Laramie Nelson was waiting the next morning, his bags problem on the table between them, he and Brock Peters had a meeting in the Washington Pinkerton office. With maps and scratch pads, they went over the situation. Peters had marked on the map the locations of the two robberies, and how the gold had probably been transported, at least for a short distance.

"There's a new railroad into Nevada, of course," Peters said, "and a spur line to Virginia City. Or a few miles from it."

"You think the gold may have been put on that line?"

"It's a strong possibility. Gold weighs like the very devil. A mule's got to be fed and watered and can't carry much very fast."

Peters then filled him in on the political situation in Nevada. "A governor's election is coming up and the Federal Government is not favorable to Fred Royal's election. But Royal seems to be the strongest candidate."

"What's that got to do with it?"

"I'm just telling you about Nevada. We don't know if there's any connection. However, the President did mention politics and Nevada has politics and politicians. Nevada also has outlaw gangs. A lot of young hellions from the war have settled there. There's armed robbery, confidence games and crooked gambling. Everything goes."

Laramie nodded, suppressing his impatience. Peters would get to the point sooner or later.

"I think you ought to go in as a gunfighter on the run. We can arrange a few posters and wanted notices."

"Don't make the rewards too high. Some eager gunfighter might want to collect. I'll be busy enough without watching my back."

"All right. We'll leave it vague. But you'll go in as a wanted man. You'll contact the biggest, most powerful outlaw gang in the area and keep your ears open. We'll arrange some method of communication, maybe a cipher, but you'll be on your own mostly. I'll have a man in Virginia City by the time you get there."

The next morning Laramie Nelson was on the train to Chicago, still in city clothes. He had a packet from Peters. There was a simple substitution cipher for any written messages, the note with it saying, "Memorize and destroy."

There was a signal for recognizing the Pinkerton operative in Virginia City, two fingers to the hatbrim, casually, or the phrase, "I have a letter for..." There was also in the packet a small stack of money totaling two hundred dollars and a typically terse note, "Account for it."

Laramie tried to sleep. He changed trains in Chicago for Omaha. His clothes were looking shabby. There was no time in Omaha for a bath. The cars were drafty and cold. There was a great deal of snow still on the Rockies.

When he arrived in Virginia City late in the afternoon, Laramie was sorely in need of a bath, and he had several days growth of beard. All this made him grumpy. But at least he was beginning to look the part of a man on the run.

A cold wind blew along the bustling streets of the town. Laramie had no heavy coat, and the icy fingers stabbed inside his jacket. The dust of the street hung high above the store buildings, dimming the slanting rays of the sun.

He got his luggage together, a carpet bag and a cheap suitcase, and hired a light rig to take him to the Turner House.

Virginia City had grown since his last visit; it was booming. New, raw-timbered structures stood next to others unpainted and shabby with weather. Dust devils whirled in the streets, spooking horses occasionally, men shouting at them profanely. Several men, faces pinched and raw with cold, stared at him from beside a horse trough.

The main street thronged with miners, cowboys, gamblers, mule skinners. There were few women to be seen. From up the street two quick shots sounded. Not so much as a head was turned.

Laramie gave the wagon driver a fifty-cent piece and went into the Turner House with his bags. He had arrived, he felt tired, slightly quarrelsome, and for just a moment wished he was somewhere else. He had a sour feeling about this assignment.

But as long as he was here, he had to start playing his new role.

He had thought it over and settled on the character he would play. He would be mean, aggressive, the kind of man gold thieves might be interested in. He would be a wanted man, handy with firearms and a knife, willing to sell his skills to the highest bidder.

The desk clerk ignored him when he leaned on the desk. Glancing around the lobby, Laramie saw that he had a good audience, including several women. The

141

women were dressed in fashionable clothes. They were either wives of important men or barroom tarts.

He said quietly, "I'd like to register, please."

The middle-aged clerk continued to ignore him.

Without a word Laramie reached over the counter, gathered a handful of shirt, yanked the clerk across the desk and dumped him onto the floor. The clerk yowled, feet thumping the desk, and he swore mightily when he hit the thin carpet. There was instant silence in the lobby.

Laramie said, in a quiet but menacing voice, "I said I wanted to register."

He leaned on the desk again and watched as the clerk scrambled to his feet and scurried around the desk. He turned the register with shaking hands. The room remained silent, and the scratching of the pen was loud as Laramie signed: *John Moduc.*

The clerk gave him a key. Laramie picked up his bags and stalked away without a word. As he started up the stairs, the chatter began again behind him. He had, he thought, made a very good beginning. It was all he could do to keep from smiling.

In the morning, refreshed by a bath and eight hours sleep, Laramie stared out over the roof tops of Virginia City as he dressed slowly. The first order of business was clothes. He couldn't go about in dude clothes and expect to get anywhere. Besides, it was uncomfortable wearing a gun in a shoulder holster when he was used to it on his hip. Also, he didn't look particularly menacing the way he was.

It took two hours to buy blue jeans, shirts and a fine leather vest with pearl buttons. Recalling Peters' note, Laramie carefully collected bills of sale. He found a heavy coat that suited him, buckled on his own gun, slid a knife into his boot and walked out onto the main street. It was a cool day, crisp and dry, the wind gone this morning.

The Grand Circle Saloon was the largest in town. It was a cavernous place and chilly, despite the four large iron stoves he could see. There were two long bars, one to his left and one at the rear, and tables for talk and cards, and any number of gaming devices. There was a stage to his right, with a brown curtain behind dark footlights. Even this early, a half dozen fancy-dressed girls and perhaps a dozen customers were in the place.

The next problem was making contact with the men who were stealing government gold. Laramie had no idea who they were or where they might be found. It wasn't going to be easy.

He crossed to the bar on his left, leaning on it, his glance raking the room. He ordered whiskey and sipped it. He had to draw attention to himself and hope the men he was after would want to hire his gun. The best way to do that would be to tackle the local bully. Every town had at least one.

A girl sidled up to him. Her narrow face was heavily rouged, her perfume strong. She looked to be in her thirties. Laramie, knowing how this life aged a woman, shaved ten years off that.

Wise black eyes appraised him.

"Hello, I'm Clara. You're new in town, ain't you?"

"Yeah, I am. Johnny Moduc. Can I buy you a drink?"

Clara nodded and crooked a finger at the barkeep.

Laramie said, "It's quiet."

"It's not yet noon. Wait until tonight. Are you a gambling man, Mr. Moduc?"

"Call me Johnny. Yeah, I gamble a little. I do a little of everything. I'm looking for some of that kind of work to do right now."

"A little of everything?" She smiled tentatively. "Are you good with that gun you're toting?"

"As good as most. Who's the best in town?"

"Well, that depends, I guess. Some say Candy Kesson."

"Interesting name. He has a sweet disposition, I suppose?"

Clara tittered. "He eats candy all the time. Some call him the Candy Kid. He's usually in here evenings, anyone can point him out."

Laramie nodded. The place was about like any other frontier saloon and dance hall. Three or four hardcases stood by the door looking over the room, half drunkenly. In the far corner an incipient fight had started which was soon broken up. It was too early in the day, Laramie decided, for serious brawls; a lot more rotgut would have to flow before that happened.

One of the dance hall girls was half indignantly, half coquettishly pulling up the shoulder strap which one of the riders had disarranged.

Laramie Nelson spotted a man he thought to be the bouncer, a hulking man with a broken nose, cauliflower ears, a gun on his hip. He was leaning on the far end of the bar reading a newspaper.

Laramie jerked his head. "Who's the bouncer?"

"Joe Lidski. Don't tangle with him, Johnny."

Laramie smiled tightly. "Mean?"

"Real mean. Nobody gives him trouble. Not even Candy."

144

"I think I'll try my luck," Laramie said, motioning toward the faro layout.

Clara had been a help, but he didn't wish to get involved with her. She pouted as he moved away from her, then looked around the room for another prospect.

Laramie played for a half hour and managed to lose ten dollars.

He shrugged ruefully and turned away from the table. He waved at Clara across the room and left the saloon, wondering if Peters would allow him to charge off the ten dollars loss to expenses.

He would be back tonight to tangle purposely with Joe Lidski. At least the bouncer was wearing a gun. That would make it ideal for Laramie's purpose.

Laramie Nelson resumed his inspection of Virginia City, made a deal to hire a sorrel horse by the week, and returned to the hotel for supper. After a cigarette on the veranda he retired to his room to clean, oil and reload his six-shooter. He spent an hour in practice before the room's cloudy mirror; he hadn't done much gun handling for several weeks. Soon the gun was as much a part of him as his right hand.

It wasn't speed that won most gunfights, but accuracy, unless the shoot-out took place across a card table. In that case a man with a big, heavy Colt was at a disadvantage if he faced a gambler palming a little .41 derringer.

With Joe Lidski he would depend on both speed and accuracy. He wanted to impress those watching with his speed, and he had no desire to kill Lidski. He could make

145

his point by simply outdrawing the man. Laramie hoped Candy Kesson would be there to see it. He had made discreet inquiries around town about the Candy Kid and had learned that the youth, barely twenty-one, was respected and feared.

Laramie entered the Grand Circle in the middle of the evening. As Clara had said, it was a busy place. There were at least a hundred men at the two bars, the tables and clotted around the gaming layouts. There were four bartenders on duty, all sweating heavily and harried. Over a dozen painted girls circulated or perched on laps, their laughter high and shrill. Laramie didn't see Clara anywhere.

It was a boomtown atmosphere, loud, raucous, frenetic. Laramie had seen other boomtowns, where the rich ore seem to pour out of the earth in an inexhaustible flood, and the men engaged in digging it out spent their earnings as though it would indeed last forever.

He didn't see Joe Lidski right away. Finally he spotted the bouncer coming from one of the card rooms, those reserved for special and important guests. Lidski came out for only a moment, then re-entered the room.

Laramie bought a stein of beer and sat on one of the wooden benches to watch the stage show. The girls singing and dancing were loud if nothing else. They received scant attention, the bulk of the audience more intent on gambling. The show went on for nearly an hour before the finale, a boisterous cancan number.

Laramie returned to the bar with the empty stein just as the card room door opened and Lidski emerged. The man came directly to the bar, stopping alongside Laramie.

Laramie dropped the empty stein on the bouncer's foot.

Lidski yowled, hopping about on one foot, trying to yank his boot off. His anger seemed all out of proportion to the "accident." Then his baleful gaze focused on Laramie, and he charged, swinging both fists like clubs.

Laramie might easily have been downed, the fight over before it began, if the bouncer's footwork hadn't been impaired by his injured foot. Laramie rolled along the bar, ducking under the man's attack, and managed to avoid the bruising fists.

He stuck out a foot and tripped Lidski. The man screamed curses, stumbling to one knee. Laramie said loudly, "It was an accident, mister. What you taking on so for?"

"I'll kill you!" Lidski said through gritted teeth. That was all he said. He came up off the floor swinging again, wilder now as his rage mounted.

Laramie ducked and weaved and threw several swift punches that drew blood from Lidski's beefy face. It had been a lucky break, the chance to drop the stein. Now he didn't have to pick a fight openly. Now the crowd was with him, believing him to be the one picked on. The circumstances could hardly be better, except that he now faced the rough task of stopping Lidski cold.

Lidski's temper was running out of control. One of his long arms swept up a bottle from the bar; he hurled it at Laramie and it smashed into a table. A woman's scream rose above the clamor. The two of them were contained now in a wide, loose circle of men, all watching the fight with glee. No one tried to stop it. With a small part of his mind Laramie noted the cheers, the shouts of encouragement, the bets being made as to the outcome.

For several moments Laramie was busy dodging Lidski's mad, bull-like rushes, and ducking the clubbing, roundhouse swings. He was sure that soon Lidski's temper would cool somewhat and he would settle into a machine-like efficiency and beat him to a pulp.

Laramie began taunting the man in an attempt to keep his anger at a boil. He called Lidski contemptuous names in a cutting voice.

Then Lidski made the move Laramie had been waiting for. His rage at white heat, he snatched at the revolver at his belt.

Instantly Laramie drew and fired, his hand a blur of speed. He aimed low, the bullet slamming into the bouncer's leg. He yelped and fell to the floor, his own shot splintering the planks at his feet.

Laramie jumped in close and kicked the gun out of Lidski's hand. The fight went out of the bouncer. He lay moaning, clutching at his leg with both hands, and rocking in agony.

Men crowded around Laramie, wanting to shake his hand, wanting to buy him drinks. One said, "I been hoping someone would do that."

Apparently Joe Lidski was not the most popular man in town.

Laramie was scarcely touched, a bruised cheek, a cut lip. Several men gathered around the big bouncer and carried him into a back room. A doctor was sent for.

Laramie smiled, thanking the gladhanders. "I don't wish to seem unsociable, gents, but I don't want the marshal to get too good a look at me neither."

A man took his arm. "Come this way then."

Laramie was escorted to a rear door and sent on his way with a pat on the back. He made his way down a delivery alley to the street and back to his hotel room. His mission had been accomplished. If the fight didn't bring him to the attention of the wagon train looters, probably nothing else would.

He was not too surprised by a rap on his door a few minutes later. He drew his pistol. "Who is it?"

"I have a letter for Mr. Moduc."

The prearranged signal with one of the Pinkerton men.

Holding the pistol down by his thigh, Laramie opened the door. The man standing in the hallway was short and slight, wearing poor clothes and shabby boots, with several days growth of beard stubbling his narrow features.

Laramie said, "Who's the letter from?"

The man pushed past him with a quick glance down the hall. "Brock Peters, for hell's sake!"

Locking the door, Laramie grinned. "I had to be sure. You don't look like much."

"Don't judge me by the whiskers. I'm Frank Allison." He smiled thinly. "I heard you had a fight tonight. I'm sorry I didn't see it."

"He would have clobbered me with his fists. I had to shoot him in the leg. What do you have for me?"

"Not much. I'll tell you all I know, and you can ask questions. We don't have what you could call a lead."

"I've heard of someone called Candy Kesson."

"A very slick article. Candy is a gunman, and a fair thinker, too. He's small and young, but deadly as a sidewinder. The word is he's killed at least a dozen men and he's hardly twenty. We believe he works for a man named Nat Colton. Colton is a political insider. He's very close to Fred Royal and the talk is that he'll be Royal's right hand man if Royal is elected governor."

Laramie frowned. "I don't quite get the connection between this political angle and the gold shipment robberies."

Allison scratched his beard. "Neither do I." He smiled. "I reckon that's your job."

"If there is a connection. Is Candy the biggest outlaw in these parts?"

"I don't know about that, but he pulls a lot of weight for a young fella. He seems to ramrod a lot of men, and it took quite a few to move that gold as smoothly as it was done."

"Any idea yet as to what happened to the gold?"

"None. I figure it's still around somewhere, the bulk of it. It's too heavy to move far without attracting some attention."

Laramie paced back and forth. He was restless, itching for action. This way he just seemed to be marking time. He glanced at Allison and had to grin.

"Just what are you supposed to be in that get-up besides a saddle tramp?"

Allison said cheerfully, "That's it. I'm a bum. I came in on a freight, and I've been picking up odd jobs for a week now, keeping my eyes and ears open, for all the good it's done me. I can't go to the telegraph office without arousing suspicion, of course, so I'll have to contact you if I turn up anything. But it looks like it's mostly up to you."

"Are you eating?"

Allison scratched blunt fingers through the beard and signed deeply. "I'm trying to look underfed. It ain't easy not eating with money in my boot." He squinted at Laramie. "A word of warning. Watch out for that Lidski. He's meaner than a sack of snakes and he'll think you made a fool of him in front of his friends. My hunch is he'll even be fired."

"Is he connected with Candy Kesson?"

"Not that I know of."

Laramie took another turn around the room. "Where does this Candy hang out?"

"In town somewhere. I've seen him in the Grand Circle and other saloons, usually with several hangers-on. I can't follow him out of town because I'd be through if I'm seen on a horse."

"Candy isn't wanted for anything then?"

"Not that I've been able to learn." Allison got to his feet. "I'd better drift. How'll we keep in touch?"

"I'll have a horse stabled in the livery across the street. It seems a good place to meet. We could talk in one of the stalls, as though you're panhandling me. I might even spare you a dime. I doubt Peters would approve more than that on the expense sheet."

Allison laughed. "Put two fingers to your hat if you have anything and I'll do the same."

Allison left the room quickly.

A short while later, Laramie was sitting on the bed about to remove his boots when there was a sharp rap on the door.

"Who is it?"

The voice in the hall was muffled. "Desk clerk."

The pistol held down by his thigh, Laramie opened the door. He was confronted by two men with drawn weapons pointed at his chest.

"Back in the room," one said.

Laramie Nelson backed up a few steps. The two men came in and shut the door. One, lean and dark, with brown hair hanging below his ears, stood with his back against the door. The other, the man who had spoken, was stocky, with a tough face and hard eyes that squinted slightly. He said, "You're Moduc?"

Laramie shrugged, grinning to himself. Well, he'd been itching for action. Now it looked like it was coming his way. He might be able to outgun the pair, but that would defeat his purpose. He dropped the pistol onto the bed. "I'm Moduc."

"Candy wants to see you," the stocky man said.

"Now?"

"Of course now!"

Laramie pretended reluctance. "Can't it wait until tomorrow?"

"Now, not tomorrow." The man motioned with his gun. "Candy wants a friendly visit."

"Yeah, I can see that," Laramie said dryly.

He strapped on his gunbelt, slipped on his coat and hat. The dark man opened the door and stayed behind to blow out the lamp. They went down the stairs single file, Laramie in the lead.

Virginia City sprawled in Gold Canyon, the place where the first gold discoveries had been made. Candy was staying near the edge of town in a squat, square house of brick and clapboard. A full moon rode high overhead, flooding the landscape with light. To the north, the hills, pitted and scarred by pockets and tunnels made by miners in search of ore, were clearly visible.

At their knock the door was opened by a slim, towheaded youth, with a round, genial face. He looked about as dangerous as a playful puppy. It was only when he turned into the splash of lamplight that Laramie saw his eyes, cold and gray as slate.

The youth held out his hand. "I'm Bob Kesson. They call me Candy."

"Johnny Moduc." Candy's hand was small, but it showed surprising strength.

Laramie looked around the room. It wasn't richly furnished—a turkey carpet on the floor, a mirror and several dismally dark pictures on the walls, a few sticks of furniture.

Candy took a horehound candy from his pocket and popped it into his mouth. "I saw your tussle with Joe Lidski. Pretty good."

"Any fight's good if you can get out of it in one piece."

"I also hear," Candy said innocently, "that you're not real anxious to meet up with lawmen."

Laramie squinted at him, then glanced back at the two men still in the doorway. He said curtly, "I'm not wanted in Nevada."

"Me neither!"

Candy's laughter was infectious, and Laramie found himself instinctively liking the youth.

Candy sobered. "Let's see how good you are with that iron you're toting." He strode to a side door and motioned outside.

"In the dark?" Laramie asked in astonishment.

"Moon's bright enough for me." Candy's grin was wolfish. "Time's a man has to shoot in the dark."

The stocky man followed them outside. The only outbuilding visible was a small barn. A bluff loomed darkly behind it.

"Toss one, Squint."

The man called Squint stooped over a wooden crate half filled with bottles. Standing again, he tossed a bottle high into the air. Moonlight glinted off the spinning glass.

Laramie drew his Colt, thumbing back the hammer, and smashed the bottle cleanly at the top of its trajectory. The sound of the shot echoed back from the bluff.

Candy looked at him with respect.

"Not bad. I understand you're looking for a job. Moduc. That right?"

"A man has to eat."

"Squint!"

Squint flung another bottle high. Laramie's hand flashed, the Colt boomed, and shards of glass fell around them. Laramie ejected the two shell cases and reloaded.

Candy held out his hand, and Squint gave him a bottle. "I'm a sort of strawboss for a man named Nat Colton. Ever hear of him?"

"Don't think so."

Candy flipped the bottle without warning, only a few feet above the ground. Laramie's shot shattered it.

Candy grunted.

"Not bad." His head swung around, his gaze pinning Laramie. "Looks to me like Lidski got off easy."

"I didn't want to kill him."

"Could be a bad mistake. Lidski's a backshooter." He gestured toward the house. "This place belongs to Nat Colton. He's over to Carson City right now with Fred Royal. An election's coming up. Guess you heard about that?"

"I read something about. I'm not much for politics."

Candy pulled a thin cigar from his pocket, rolled the end between his lips and struck a match. He said, "You ever handle men? I mean, were you in the war maybe?"

"I was."

"How many men?"

Laramie shrugged. "Thirty, maybe forty."

"That so?" Candy's look was sly. "You join up or did they get you."

"They got me," Laramie lied. "I was on my way to the

border. Man says he was short of cavalrymen. I left the army first foggy night."

Candy nodded to Squint, holding up two fingers.

Squint tossed two bottles into the air. Candy drew and fired twice, one shot following the other so closely they sounded almost as one. Both bottles were hit at the top of their arcs.

Candy holstered his gun without glancing at the shattered glass and started back toward the house as the echoes of the shots were still bouncing off the bluff, throwing away his cigar.

Laramie was impressed. Candy could handle a gun, no doubt about that. His draw had been lightning fast, smooth as silk. Laramie had to wonder how he'd fare against the youngster if he ever had to draw against him.

Inside, Kesson scooped up several hard candies from a box and popped them into his mouth. "If you're looking for a job, I think I've got something for you." They were alone now, the two men outside somewhere.

"What kind of a job?" Laramie asked.

"You that particular?"

Laramie grinned crookedly. "I don't wait on tables."

Candy lowered his voice slightly. "One of our problems is finding men who are both fighters and who can think. You'd be surprised how few of that kind are around. I've seen you in a fight, and I know you can handle a gun. But I don't know how good you can think."

"I've been in some tight spots. Sometimes I shot my way out, other times I've had to think my way out. I'm still alive and kicking."

Candy smiled thinly. "What you wanted for?"

Laramie shrugged. "Robbing folks, this and that." He slapped his pistol. "This here's my meal ticket and I've lived pretty high on the hog with it."

All of a sudden Candy seemed to make up his mind. "All right. I think you can cut it. We'll go see Nat Colton over to Carson. I have to come right back. You'll probably be staying around awhile."

Laramie strode to the window, looking down the canyon at the town. Virginia City was built on the side of a mountain, with the railroad depot down below. It was a shabby town; low frame buildings, tents, sheds hastily thrown together, and lines of privies. There were long, low buildings with smokestacks and flumes and below, near the railroad tracks, gray mounds of crushed quartz.

It was a dismal picture. He would be glad to get away to Carson City. And it looked like things were finally beginning to move. Excitement gripped him.

I'll have to get in touch with Allison, he thought absently; *let him know where I'm going.*

He turned. "When do I leave?"

"We'll take the train in the morning."

Candy accompanied him to the door and stepped outside with him. He started to speak, and then, with shocking suddenness, he rammed his shoulder into Laramie, sending him reeling against the wall.

At almost the same moment Laramie saw a splash of orange flame blossom out by the road, something thudded into the wall at the exact spot where he had been standing a moment ago, and the sound of a shot roared.

Before Laramie could recover his balance, Candy had drawn his gun and fired twice. A scream sounded, and a hulking figure staggered into the oblong of light thrown by the open door, collapsing into the dirt face down almost at their feet.

156

They walked over to the prone figure. Candy turned the body over with the toe of his boot. It was Joe Lidski, face slack in death.

"Told you it was a mistake not to kill him when you had a chance," Candy said dryly.

Laramie drew a deep breath. "You must have sharp eyes, seeing in the dark like that, even with the moon out."

"Some people say I'm part cat."

"I reckon I owe you my life. Thanks." Laramie put out his hand.

Candy took it, grinning engagingly. "My pleasure."

As Laramie started off, Candy called after him. "I'll be knocking on your door with the chickens, Johnny. We'll have time for breakfast before the train leaves for Carson."

Laramie Nelson was waiting the next morning, his bags packed, when the Candy Kid knocked on his door. Laramie had been out earlier and contacted Allison, informing the operative of the trip to Carson City and the upcoming meeting with Colton.

"I'll follow you to Carson," Allison had said. "Soon as I can hitch a ride on a freight wagon."

Laramie and Candy had breakfast in the hotel dining room. As they ate steak and eggs, Laramie leafed through a local paper. "I see the governor's race is heating up."

"It figures to."

"What kind of a man is this Royal?"

Candy shrugged slim shoulders. "All right, I guess. I've only met him a couple of times. He's well liked around the state and rich. Owns a big ranch out of Carson a ways and a couple of good paying mines. Colton's my boss. I take my orders from him."

Laramie folded his paper and tried to sound casual. "Just how does Colton figure in?"

"He's worked for Fred Royal for some time and it's my guess he's slated for a top spot in the government if Royal's elected."

"You worked for Colton long, Candy?"

"Not long. A year." Candy lit one of his thin cigars and looked at Laramie through eyes narrowed by the drift of smoke. "Where you from, Johnny?"

Laramie didn't welcome the change of subject, but he knew it was far too early to press hard for information. It could easily arouse Candy's suspicions. "I came west from the river towns along the Big Muddy. I found it a bit healthier farther west." He finished his coffee and rolled a cigarette. "What time is the train?"

"We have just enough time to make it."

The train to Carson City wasn't crowded, and they found two seats together in the coach car. Although the railroad had reached Virginia City only a short time ago, the railroad cars were old, uncomfortable, the seats hard and well-worn, the floors stained with tobacco juice. The floor of the one in which Laramie and Candy rode swirled with debris at every gust of wind.

Laramie managed to question Candy again, making it all seem the natural curiosity of a man new to the territory and undertaking a new job.

Colton, according to Candy, was a powerful man, a leader of men and destined for better things. "He's got more gumption in his little finger than Fred Royal has in his whole body!"

"I gather you don't think much of Royal?"

"I don't. He's got the money, but he's wishywashy. I swear I don't see what people see in that man. Of course," he said cautiously, "I only know what I hear, like I already told you. I ain't acquainted with him much personal." Then he brightened, grinning. "But his wife, now there's a woman!"

Diana Royal, according to Candy, was a willful but beautiful female.

Laramie used the newspaper he'd bought in Virginia City to raise the subject of the gold shipment robberies. "It says here they haven't caught the bandits yet."

Candy snorted. "And they ain't likely to neither!"

"What makes you say that?"

Candy turned cautious again. "They're no closer to them now than in the beginning. That tells you something, don't it?"

Laramie made his voice wistful. "That certainly was a pile of money. I'd like to have a chance at it."

"Stick around." Candy grinned slyly. "You just might get that chance."

Laramie said carefully, "What do you mean?"

"You'll have to wait and see," Candy said enigmatically.

Laramie had to be content with that for the time being.

He scrubbed his jaw, thinking hard. Running a political campaign took money, he'd always heard. Had Colton stole the money to finance Royal's campaign for governor? It didn't seem too likely, not if Royal was as rich as Candy had indicated.

Laramie rolled a cigarette and smoked thoughtfully. Maybe Colton was stealing the gold for purposes of his own. Somehow, Laramie had a strong hunch that Colton

159

and Candy Kesson were behind the robberies, and Colton was in Carson. Maybe the gold was there, too.

He might very well be heading right to it.

Candy had put out his cigar and was dozing, his head lolling back on the seat. For some time Laramie had been noticing Army troops spaced along the railroad tracks at regular intervals. He mentioned this to Candy.

Candy stretched, yawning. "The Army's been moving men into the area in numbers since the last holdup."

Laramie's interest quickened. "You mean another gold shipment's going out soon? By rail this time?"

Candy grinned lazily. "Now how would I know about that, Johnny boy?"

The train was pulling into Carson City. Although Carson was the state capital, it wasn't as bustling as Virginia City, the people on the streets less boisterous, more soberly dressed. Laramie guessed that most of them were somehow connected with the state government.

Candy hired a buggy to drive them out to Royal's ranch about five miles out of town.

It was an impressive spread. There was a big brick house, stables and corrals, a long bunkhouse, and a smaller house behind the big one where Candy took Laramie. It was more private, Candy explained; the big house was full of people coming and going with election business.

Candy left Laramie cooling his heels and was alone with Colton for a half hour before Laramie was ushered in and introduced to Colton. Candy left the two men alone.

Colton was a small man of about forty, but domineering, energetic. His hair was bright red, his eyes a cold, pale blue. His movements were quick, decisive. He was something of a dandy, with a military flavor about his manner and his clothing.

160

Colton said, "Candy has been telling me about you, Moduc."

"All good, I hope."

"Not only today." Colton said curtly. "He wired me yesterday from Virginia City and I've had you checked out."

Laramie was slightly surprised by the man's frankness.

He was even more surprised when Colton opened the roll-top desk and took out a thin sheaf of wanted posters. The top one described one Johnny Moduc, wanted for murder in Louisiana.

Laramie grunted, shrugging. Brock Peters had done his work well.

"I have to know who I'm dealing with," Colton said.

"Yeah, I reckon you do."

Colton smiled meagerly, his military manner relaxing a trifle. He put the posters carefully back into the desk and closed it. "There's no need for me to telegraph Louisiana, but I am surprised you haven't changed your name."

Laramie wondered if that was a subtle threat or a warning. He said, "I didn't bother because I didn't know the poster was still out on me." He drummed his fingers on the butt of his Colt. "I'll change it right now."

"A good idea." Colton nodded crisply. "To what?"

"Uh . . . Johnny Morgan."

"Hmmmm," Colton said. "I knew a gunnie once named Morgan. The so-and-so let himself be drygulched by a stinking sheepherder. But it'll be a good name for you." He took a cigar from a box on his desk without offering Laramie one. "I'm going to send you out to Bill Jessop. He'll show you what we're doing here."

Colton stared at him, pale eyes appraising. "Fred Royal's going to be next governor of this state, but it's a

161

state in great disorder. The booming mines have attracted all sorts of drifters and riffraff. Policing in most areas in the state is a big joke."

"Policing?" Laramie said, taken aback.

Colton said forcibly, "I'm building a force of Regulators, the same as the Rangers down in Texas. They're needed here. They'll have regular police powers, acting under me."

Laramie listened, astonished. Of all the things he had been expecting, a private police force was the last thing in his mind. Was Colton building up his own private army?

Colton was saying, "We must have law and order in Nevada, and Royal agrees with me. This is the quickest way of getting it. But we need men to lead. Candy thinks you're the kind of man we're looking for? Are you?"

Laramie rubbed his chin, not wishing to appear too eager to join a police group. He finally said, "I wasn't exactly planning on joining up with some law force."

"You won't be sorry," Colton said. "That's all I can tell you for now. Except I'll start you at three hundred a month and found."

Laramie detected the emphasis on "found" and three hundred a month was three times what a good law officer earned. He said, "Deal me in."

Colton's meager smile flickered. "You're smart. We're going to have to use smart men, I can tell you. Come along." He opened the door and ushered Laramie out. "We'll have a drink on it. There're some people I want you to meet."

He led Laramie across to the big house. Laramie didn't see Candy anywhere. He asked about him.

"Candy had to hurry back to Virginia City," Colton said. "He asked me to pass on his apologies and he'll be seeing you before long."

In the big house a group of people were gathered around a couple, a man and a woman. Colton introduced them as Fred and Diana Royal. Laramie saw a slight, graying man, stooped and older than he would have thought. Yet his grip was surprisingly firm. "Welcome, Mr. Morgan."

Diana was younger, vibrant, quite dark and very lovely. Laramie felt his face flush slightly. She was everything Candy had said she would be. Laramie could see that Nat Colton thought so, too. Colton never strayed far from her side.

A servant came around with wine, and Laramie drank, basking in Diana's smiles.

"You're from the east, Mr. Morgan?"

"Yes. St. Louis, New Orleans..."

"I love New Orlenas," she said wistfully. "It's so different from this desert and these brown hills." She grimaced and turned to her husband. "Have you finished your business?"

"Yes, my dear."

"Then let's go." She smiled at Laramie. "We have to go into Carson." She said a few words to the others and then swept out of the room, trailed by her husband.

Laramie saw Colton looking after Royal with an amused, somewhat patronizing smile on his narrow face.

When the Royals had gone, Nat Colton raised his glass. "To Governor Royal," he said with a straight face.

They all laughed.

Bill Jessop had about a hundred and fifty men training in a military-style camp set up on the ranch.

Jessop was a big, blustery man; he had a thick head of black hair and piercing gray eyes. He had been a major in the Confederate Cavalry, serving under Joe Wheeler.

"We've got agents out," he told Laramie, "scouring the countryside for more men. We hope to put 'em all in proper uniform soon. You were with the South, sir?"

"I tried to be," Laramie lied. "But I was waylaid by the Unions and forced into a unit. I got out quick as I could."

Jessop snorted, shaking his big head. "Infernal nerve! That's the North for you!"

Jessop showed him around the camp, perhaps sixty tents laid out in neat rows. There were also several huts for officers and two cook shacks. Beyond the huts were corrals where dust was rising from a hundred or more milling horses. And from the other side of the corrals came the howls and yells of many men, some giving orders, some swearing.

"The men are drilling," Jessop said proudly. "You'll be sharing a hut with Lieutenant Barnes, who happens to be away on assignment at the moment."

It was little more than a clapboard shack, with two bunk beds, a small square mirror, pegs on the walls for hanging clothes, one bench and a Franklin stove for heat. A lantern hung on a nail.

Fred Royal, Laramie thought, must be sure of winning his election. Or Nat Colton. He remembered Colton's mocking toast and the knowing grins. There was something stirring under the surface here, something dark and evil.

Laramie took possession of the hut, then attended a staff meeting where he met two other officers. He was assigned a troop and given the title of lieutenant. He would be furnished a horse and given a uniform when they were ready. Although the discipline was less severe than that of a military camp, it was like one in most other respects.

At midnight Allison came rapping on his door.

Laramie was surprised. "How'd you get into the camp? It's supposed to be guarded."

"Not all that well." Allison grinned. He still looked like a saddle tramp. "You forget I'm an experienced forager. The guards are in a card game right now."

Laramie lit a stump of candle, setting it on the floor. "How'd you get to Carson?"

"Begged a ride on an Army train. They're patrolling the tracks between here and Virginia City. What's going on here?"

"I haven't learned much yet. I've signed on as a Regulator. Colton calls this bunch the Regulators. He's organizing a military force to police the state when Royal's elected. Or so he says."

Allison scratched his bearded chin, frowning. "Then you're on the wrong side, ain't you?"

"I'm not sure. There's some connection between Colton and the Candy Kid, I don't know what yet. I strongly suspect Candy ramrods the gold robberies, yet he works for Colton. And Colton is the power behind Royal."

"That's the talk I hear."

"Since the Army is patrolling the tracks, it looks like they're going to ship the gold by train the next time. If so, they're certainly not keeping it a secret."

"The Army commander thinks he's got enough men in the area now not to have to resort to trickery or secrecy again." Allison frowned. "This bunch of Regulators or whatever—do you think they're being used in the gold raids?"

"I doubt it. Most of the men, including the commander, a man named William Jessop, are ex-Confederates. They're not outlaws, just ex-soldiers in a lost cause and spoiling for a fight." Laramie rolled a cigarette as he talked. "But I have a feeling Nat Colton is tied in somewhere. That's why I took this job, figuring to be close to headquarters."

"It may tie you down too much."

Laramie nodded, smoking thoughtfully. "There's that. Allison, if the next gold shipment goes by train, what do you think are the chances?"

"In my opinion?" Allison's eyes twinkled. "In a word, poor. If you think about the other two robberies . . . Slick, well-planned jobs. The gent commanding the Army isn't the smartest. I think he could be fooled somewhere, any of a hundred ways."

Laramie sighed, scowling down at the yellow, flickering candle beginning to sputter in its own grease. He was one man caught in a web of intrigue; he felt squeezed by the power plays going on about him. On one side by the Army and the Federal Government, on another by Candy Kesson and his riders, and on the third by the private army of Nat Colton.

And there was always Brock Peters, ready to come down on him like a house if the assignment wasn't carried out successfully. It wasn't the sort of job he relished. He wished now that he had said no to the President. But what kind of a man turns down the President of his country?

Allison broke into his thoughts. "There's one other thing."

Laramie looked up. "What's that?"

"A rumor, may be nothing more than that. I heard it from a drunk, and he heard it in the back room of one of Carson's finest emporiums . . ."

"What is it?" Laramie demanded impatiently.

Allison held up his hand. "I'm merely telling you what I

heard, mind. It's hard to swallow. My drunken friend was supposed to be passed out and overheard two men talking. Nat Colton will wait until Royal is elected governor, then kick him out and take over."

Laramie stared. "You mean, take over the state by force?"

"I told you it's hard to swallow."

"What else?"

"That's all. My friend, the drunk, was noticed and booted out into the alley."

Laramie was silent, thinking. A story overheard by a drunk. Yet it could explain a lot of things. Colton's private army, for instance. He asked, "How about the cavalry? How many are there?"

"Four troops, none of them at full strength. I'd guess about two hundred altogether."

"How many in Virginia City?"

"I don't know. I'd guess maybe a hundred on patrol along the railroad line, maybe more. That leaves less than a hundred in Virginia City. If you're thinking how many troops on the gold train, probably fifty. The commander will think that's enough, what with the troops patrolling the tracks. Unless he can be convinced there's more of a threat, and he's pretty bullheaded."

Laramie nodded. If that was true, and it probably was, then Candy and his raiders would be almost an equal match for the Army men on the train, plus the fact that the element of surprise would be on their side. And the more soldiers killed, the fewer left around to oppose Colton's take-over of the state. It was all beginning to make sense.

Allison asked, "You think I should go back to Virginia City?"

"No." Laramie snuffed out the guttering candle

between his fingers. "Best stick around Carson. See if you can keep tabs on Colton, who he meets with and so on. See if you can learn more about this scheme of his."

Allison agreed. After he had gone into the night as silently as he had come, Laramie lay awake on his bunk, hands behind his head, staring into the darkness. Colton take over a state of the Union?

It was a grandiose scheme, the plan of a madman. Yet it might work. Colton had many things going for him. The Federal Government had its hands full and was short of funds. There was only one good way to move Federal troops into Nevada quickly, by the railroad, and the railroad could be blown sky high in a hundred places.

Of course, there was one way to stop Nat Colton, Laramie thought; shoot him.

He had no orders to assassinate anyone, and he doubted if he could commit murder in cold blood, even if ordered. Anyway, he'd been sent here to learn who was stealing Nevada gold, not to foil the plans of a man bent on seizing a state for himself.

It could be the result of something a drunk had dreamed on a belly full of rotgut whiskey. The more Laramie thought about it, the more outlandish it seemed.

He finally fell into a restless slumber.

The next morning Jessop set him to drilling troops. Laramie was given a platoon, thirty-six men on horseback, and for two hours he drilled them relentlessly. He had two good sergeants, men who had learned their trade shooting at Yankees.

After the drill they rubbed down the horses, then had rifle practice until noon at a crude rifle range set up against a hillside. The midday meal consisted of soup, bread and white beans. They were given an hour to digest it.

Laramie rolled a brown cigarette and strolled back.

Snake Fisher came out of a tent and stepped directly into Laramie's path.

Laramie knew the man instantly.

His face slack with astonishment, Fisher stopped short. "I'll be damned! Laramie Nelson! What's a Pinkerton man doing here?"

Laramie Nelson could only nod. "Hello, Snake."

He had been responsible for sending Snake Fisher to prison three years back. Had the man been released or had he escaped? It didn't really matter. Snake knew him and could give the show away. Laramie supposed the man had another name, but it was easy to see why he was called Snake. His head was somewhat triangular in shape, he had a curious way of weaving his head, and his black eyes were flat, unblinking.

Recovering from his surprise, Snake said, "I'm using another handle these days. Expect you're doing the same?"

"Johnny Morgan."

Snake nodded. "Roy Douglas." He grinned. "Maybe we'd better have a little talk."

Laramie pointed out his hut. "We'd best not be seen together. I'm not supposed to know anybody here."

Snake Fisher nodded. "After supper."

Laramie was waiting when the man knocked on the hut long after dark. He had little choice but to wait. Laramie

169

had turned down the lantern and hung it on a wire by the single window which he had covered with a blanket.

Laramie latched the door after him and motioned to the bunk.

Snake sat, head weaving, smiling slyly. Laramie had a good idea what was on the man's mind. And he was right. Snake came quickly to the point.

"You want to keep me quiet. Your being here means you're what you Pinkertons call undercover, ain't it?"

Laramie waited, saying nothing.

"Well, I don't care nothing about these hombres playing soldier. I only signed on because I'm flat. You can keep me quiet easy."

"How's that?"

"Five hundred dollars."

Laramie almost smiled. "That's a lot of money. I don't have it."

"But you can get it. The Pinkertons is rich."

"Three hundred," Laramie said. "But I'll need three or four days to get it."

"Oh, I'll give you the time. But the price is five hundred. You know how it is."

Laramie sighed. "I know how it is."

Snake left, head weaving, grinning.

Laramie felt depressed. This was a complication he didn't need. He had to get into Carson City and wire Peters for the money. It galled him to pay a man like Snake Fisher, but it was necessary. Maybe it wouldn't matter five days from now if Colton knew he was a Pinkerton. Then he relaxed, smiling faintly, thinking of Peters' profane reaction at being asked to fork over five hundred dollars in bribe money.

He ran into a snag the next morning when he asked Jessop for permission to go into Carson. Jessop refused without even asking Laramie's reason for going. "You only started yesterday. Nobody, officers nor men, get leave until the weekend."

"I'll only be gone an hour or so."

"Doesn't matter. I've got my orders same as you. The answer's no."

Laramie sighed and gave up for the moment. He put his men through the morning drill, his mind gnawing at the problem. Allison had managed to get in and out without being seen, so why couldn't he?

At the rifle range he left a sergeant in charge and strolled back to the corrals. If he could slip away now, he could ride into town, send his telegram and get back by the noon meal. The chances were good he wouldn't be missed.

There was a guard lounging in the shade of the shed where the saddles were kept. There was no chance of getting a horse saddled and riding out without the guard spotting him. Laramie swore under his breath and walked toward the cook shack. He could walk, of course, but five miles to a horseman was out of the question.

He stopped short. There was a saddled horse by the cookshack.

Laramie didn't hesitate. He walked directly to the horse and gathered up the reins, leading the animal around the shack. There was considerable noise all around, but no one saw him. The camp was patrolled but not fenced.

Laramie led the horse into the brush directly behind the cookshack. In minutes he was out of sight of the camp.

He paused and listened. He heard nothing but rifle fire from the range. He looked the animal over. A weary dun, with a worn saddle.

"You're not much to get shot for, boss," he muttered, and mounted up.

It took less than an hour to reach town and get off his telegram to Peters at the Denver Pinkerton office. He saw no one he knew. He briefly debated looking up Allison, then decided against it. If he rode directly back to camp, there was a good chance his absence wouldn't have been noted.

He was halfway back when he heard the hoofbeats of racing horses on the road. Laramie turned off the road immediately, but they had already seen him, a half-dozen mounted men rounding a curve up ahead. The fact that he had tried to avoid them caused a shout. A Winchester barked, the lead streaking overhead. Laramie reined in. He didn't have the horseflesh under him for a chase.

He recognized a couple of the men as being from the camp. One shouted, "By God, we're in luck! This's him!"

Pistols covered him, and Laramie felt his hopes plummet. How had they found him out?

They took his gun, turned him about and headed back toward the Royal ranch. One man was sent on ahead to inform Nat Colton they had captured Johnny Moduc.

"What's up, gents?" Laramie asked.

"I expect you know Roy Douglas? Old friend of yours, ain't he, Mr. Pinkerton?"

"Yes, I know him," Laramie said, knowing what was coming.

"He sold you out, friend. Colton paid him more'n you promised."

They put him in a stout shack not far from the main

camp. Two men were left to guard the shack. Laramie was searched but not tied.

Lighting a match, Laramie saw that he was in a plank-floored room obviously once used for storing blasting powder. There were signs lettered *danger,* leaning against one wall, and empty boxes scattered about. There was one tiny barred window, letting in almost no light.

The guards settled down by the door outside, and Laramie could hear the murmur of this voices through the cracks between the planks.

The afternoon passed slowly, and night fell. No one came near him. The guards weren't relieved, and Laramie could hear them grumbling. He stood at the window, feeling the night breeze on his face. The window looked away from the houses and the camp, toward the hills. What would Colton do? Shoot him? Probably. A man like Colton would charge him with treason and shoot him without a qualm. But why the delay? Maybe Colton was—

Something said, "Nelson, Shhh!"

Startled, Laramie blinked, and Allison materialized out of the gloom beside the shack, grinning, a finger to his lips. The agent passed a pistol through the bars. He whispered, "Make a fuss."

Laramie took the weapon. He nodded, and Allison disappeared. Laramie wondered how Allison had learned of his predicament. But he didn't have time to ponder that now.

He pounded on the door with the butt of the pistol, evoking a snarl, "Shut up in there!"

Laramie pounded again, and kicked the door. A chain rattled, then a lock clicked. The door opened a crack, and a man said, "Step back to the far wall, mister."

Laramie tossed a stick at the wall, and the door opened wider at its clatter. Laramie was in pitch darkness, but he could see the moonlight glint off the barrel of the guard's pistol, and the silhouette of his head. The guard stepped inside warily, and Laramie hit him just behind the ear with the pistol.

The guard's own gun exploded as he fell, the bullet thudding into the far wall. The guard outside yelled. As Laramie stepped over the guard's body and slipped outside, there was a furious exchange of shots, then silence.

He saw the second guard sprawled, face down. Laramie kicked his pistol away, just in case, and ran to Allison, who was lying a few yards away.

Allison was dead.

Laramie experienced an immense sense of loss. He hadn't realized how much he had come to like the unassuming agent. He knelt by the man, anger working in him. He saw, without immediately comprehending, lights flickering on in the big house a few hundred yards distant. Someone would be investigating the shots.

He searched Allison's pockets, finding a wallet, a silver watch and an envelope. He stuffed it all into his pockets, stripped the cartridge belt from the dead man, took Allison's gun and ran in a crouch toward the big house.

There were low, adobe walls enclosing a flower garden and much shrubbery. Laramie ducked, seeing men running from the camp. A man yelled, "Fetch some lanterns!"

Laramie glanced toward the corrals. That way was cut off. Men were running to and fro. Behind him, Laramie heard shouts as they discovered the bodies. A search was being hurriedly organized. Lanterns flared up like enormous fireflies in the night, and saddles were being slapped on horses in the corrals.

Then Laramie saw Diana Royal. She had come out on the porch and was watching the excitement. She was alone and fully dressed. In a moment she was joined by her husband, who lit a cigar and stared at the activity.

Now Diana said something to her husband and went inside again. Fred Royal came off the porch and across the yard. He started as Laramie Nelson rose up beside him. "By God, sir!"

Laramie said, "It's me they're looking for, Mr. Royal."

"You know my name?" Royal squinted at him. "Are you the Pinkerton man?"

Laramie hesitated, then said, "I am, yes."

Royal took his arm and drew him quickly toward the house. "You mustn't be seen." He pushed Laramie inside, then blew out the lamp. "My wife's gone up to bed." He closed the door and locked it. "What's this all about, Mr.—What's your name, Moduc?"

"No, sir. Laramie Nelson."

Royal seemed genuinely concerned, and his actions seemed to indicate that he had no thought of giving Laramie away. Could it be he knew nothing of Nat Colton's scheme to become king of Nevada?

Royal puffed on his cigar. "I had always assumed the Pinkerton Agency was on the side of law and order, Mr. Nelson."

Taken aback, Laramie blinked. "We are, sir. That's why I'm here."

"Nat Colton accuses you of murder, treason, conspiracy and what not. I'm afraid I don't understand."

"There is a conspiracy, Mr. Royal, but not on the part of the Pinkertons."

"A conspiracy?"

"Yeah. When you are elected governor of Nevada, you will be shoved aside by Nat Colton and he will take over with the help of his Regulators."

Laramie could see the effect of his words, even in the gloom of the darkened room. Royal gasped and stepped back, his eyes widening.

"That is a monstrous charge, sir! Can you prove any of this?"

Laramie went to the window, looking out toward the hut. Men with lanterns were carrying the bodies away.

"Mr. Royal, I was sent here to look into the gold robberies. I have every reason to believe they are connected with Colton's scheme to take over the state."

"I asked for proof, not what you believe! I have known Nat Colton for a good many years!"

"At the moment proof is hard to come by." Laramie sighed and motioned toward the hut. "A very good agent was just killed out there, a man who might have supplied your proof." He paused. Now Royal was silent. "I ask you to think about Colton's little private army, his Regulators, stationed on your own land. For what purpose, Mr. Royal?"

"Why, to bring law and order back to the state. It's overrun by criminals and killers. The gold train robberies should be proof of that!"

"An army of several hundred men with their only authority coming from Nat Colton?" Laramie said softly. "An army of malcontents, bitter men mostly recruited from a lost cause, who hate the Union and would welcome a country of their own where they would no longer be the defeated enemy?"

"But I . . ." Royal was visibly shaken now. "But there

176

are Federal troops in the state."

"Very few and spread thin. Colton's Regulators could overwhelm them easily."

Royal began to pace in his agitation. "I had no idea, no blessed idea."

"I believe you, sir, but it is in your power to stop them. And there's something else. I believe that the gold robberies are paying for the Regulators."

Royal halted. "I must have proof, man, proof! Your charges are simply incredible! You're implying that Mr. Colton intends to secede from the Union and form his own private state!"

"That's it exactly."

"I simply cannot believe it! I must have time to think." Royal took a step. "Can you bring me proof, Mr. Nelson?"

"Can you supply me with a horse, sir?"

Laramie Nelson was on the run. He couldn't ride into Carson. If Colton's men caught him again, he'd probably be shot on sight. Besides, he had no reason to ride into Carson City. There was certainly no reason to pick up the five hundred to pay Snake Fisher. He could wire for help, for a replacement for Allison, but things were moving too rapidly for that.

He rode toward Virginia City. He needed proof of Colton's treasonous intentions, not only for Fred Royal, but for Brock Peters and ultimately President Grant. Laramie was sure Royal was swayed; the fact that the man had sneaked Laramie away was evidence of that. But how could he get the proof needed? For some reason his

177

thoughts swung to Candy Kesson.

The weather had turned cold and cloudly, threatening rain. The horse Royal had given him was a powerful bay, his stride eating up the miles even in the dark. Laramie followed the railroad. At several points he was challenged by an Army patrol. He managed to elude them in the darkness. They were reasonably alert, at least.

He reached Virginia City shortly before dawn. He stabled the bay and rented a room in a cheap hotel from a yawning clerk. Dead tired, Laramie removed his boots and gunbelt and went to sleep without taking off the rest of his clothes.

It was past noon and raining when he awoke. Lacking shaving equipment, or anything else, he washed as best he could and left the hotel. The rain was coming down in sheets. There was a dry goods store in the block, where he bought a poncho. Farther along was a restaurant. Not knowing how far the hunt for him had spread, Laramie kept a wary eye out. No one seemed to notice him.

As he ate breakfast in the restaurant, a troop of cavalry splashed along the muddy streets outside, rattling and clanking, the troopers swearing at the rain.

A man at the next table said, "Them boys is guarding the gold shipment going out this morning."

"Naw, that ain't till tomorrow," his table companion said.

"Then what they doing out there now?"

Laramie finished his meal and rolled a cigarette, staring morosely out at the muddy street. If it was public knowledge that a gold shipment was going out, the Army must be confident.

Or overconfident. That struck Laramie as the most likely.

He ducked his head through the poncho again, put on his hat and went out. The poncho, in addition to protecting him against the rain, offered a sort of crude disguise.

Almost at once he saw Candy Kesson.

The Candy Kid was crossing the street, picking his way delicately through the mud, head down. He stepped up onto the veranda down from Laramie and scraped the mud from his boots.

Laramie slipped into a doorway, sixgun drawn. When Candy came abreast of him, Laramie said softly, "Candy..." He showed the other the muzzle of the Colt, held under the edge of the poncho.

Candy saw him instantly. His hand started for his gun, then halted, his gaze flicking from the round muzzle up to Laramie's face. He seemed unalarmed. He said easily, "Howdy, Johnny."

He stepped into the doorway alongside Laramie, his glance raking the street. There were few passersby, and none seemed to notice anything untoward about two men huddled together in a doorway out of the rain.

"Nat Colton wired me, figgering you might head this way. I figgered different. It appears I'm wrong again. You sure took me in, Johnny." For just a moment his round face tightened dangerously. "Might even say you made me out a fool. I don't know as I like that much."

"The name's Nelson, Laramie Nelson."

"Your Pinkerton name, I'd guess?"

"Yeah." Laramie nodded. "When're you holding up the gold, Candy?"

Candy's eyes rounded. Then he laughed heartily.

"You got your brass, Johnny boy, I'll hand you that. Too bad you got to be a damn Pinkerton."

179

"I guess that depends which side of the fence you're sitting." He studied the youth in speculation. "What's going to happen when Colton takes over? Where do you fit in?"

Candy started. "What?"

Laramie smiled with inward satisfaction. His hunch was right; Candy didn't know all of Colton's plans. "You mean he doesn't bother to tell you all his plans?"

Candy's eyes became flat and cold. He reached into his pocket for a horehound candy and popped it into his mouth. "I know all the plans."

"Well now, it appears you don't," Laramie drawled. "Those Regulators of his, for instance—"

"I know about them. It's a police force for Fred Royal."

"That's what Colton tells everybody, including you. But I see it as something else. The Regulators are Colton's private army. They're not getting any police training. I see it this way. Your job is to get the gold to pay for the army, then you're through. You're a gold thief. When Colton takes over, he can't afford to have you around to point a finger at him."

Candy scowled. "Take over what? You keep saying that."

"Colton will help Royal get elected, then he'll push him out, maybe kill him, then take over the state government."

"Take over the whole state?" Candy was incredulous.

"That's the way I see it."

Candy hooted. "Johnny boy, you've been chewing loco weed! That's crazy—" Candy stopped, frowning. "If what you say is true, that makes Nat Colton a traitor!"

"That's it exactly. And he's using you. What does that make you?"

Candy snorted. "It makes me nothing but a fool for listening to you! I don't know why, but you're lying! I've never heard such—"

Laramie's attention strayed, his gaze caught by something across the street. Snake Fisher had just stepped out of the Grand Circle. He stood under the shelter of the saloon's roof, head weaving as he looked both ways along the street, as though searching for someone. A gun was strapped low on his thigh.

Laramie turned his attention back to Candy. He jabbed the snout of his Colt into the youth's belly just below the ribcage, drawing a sharp gasp.

"I'll take your gun, Candy."

He relieved Candy of his weapon and stuck it in his belt. Then he jabbed with the gun again.

"We're going to walk to your place, Candy. My gun will be in your ribs all the way, hidden under the poncho. If you so much as blink an eye without me saying so, I'll blow a hole in you big enough to drive a wagon through!"

"Walk? In this rain?" Candy said in dismay. "I don't know what you're scheming now, but why can't we ride?"

"We walk," Laramie said grimly.

Candy sighed elaborately and started along the veranda. Laramie prodded him with the Colt again. "No. Out in the street."

"In all that mud?"

"A little mud won't hurt you." Laramie twisted the gun barrel. "Move, Kid!"

They stepped out into the middle of the street. The rain was letting up a little, but they sank to the ankles with each step.

Laramie didn't once look toward the Grand Circle, yet as he walked, he felt a cold itch between his shoulder blades, and his neck began to ache from holding it rigid. Any second he expected a bullet to slam into his back.

Nothing happened.

Two blocks up the main street was the side street leading to where Candy was staying. As they turned, Laramie risked a quick glance back over his shoulder.

Snake Fisher was only a few yards back, walking fast.

A few feet into the street, Laramie snapped, "Wait up, Candy!"

He whirled, crouching. Snake was just rounding the corner. Laramie shouted, "Hold it right there, Snake!"

But Snake's gun was already out and coming up.

Laramie fired, aiming low. He didn't want the man dead. Not yet. His bullet slammed into Snake's thigh. His leg was knocked out from under him, his own shot going wild.

"What the hell—" Candy muttered.

Without answering, Laramie hurried to the man on his back in the mud. He kicked the pistol out of Snake's hand.

Snake's face was contorted in agony. He was swearing in a low monotone. When he saw Laramie bending over him, his face blanched with terror. "I didn't aim to do it, Mr. Nelson, I swear! But he, Nat Colton, he offered me more money!"

"How much did he offer you to backshoot me?"

"Not you, him!" He nodded past Laramie at Candy. "He said he'd pay a thousand dollars for him dead."

Laramie glanced up at Candy, whose face was a study in bewilderment, then back at Snake Fisher. "Candy? Why kill him; he's Colton's right hand?"

"Colton said he didn't need him anymore, said he could swing the rest hisself," Snake babbled. "Said he didn't trust the Candy Kid no more, not after sending a Pinkerton man to him. Said if he couldn't trust him now, how could he when he takes over the state?"

Laramie said tensely, "Then Colton is planning a take-over?"

"Sure, Mr. Nelson, I thought you—" Snake broke off short, eyes widening in sudden terror. "No, don't—" He started to rise.

A shot boomed out in the narrow street, and Snake Fisher fell back, a black hole appearing in his shirt over the heart.

Laramie whirled on his knees, his Colt coming up. But Candy didn't pose any threat. He stood with Snake's muddy gun smoking in his hand, gazing down at the dead man with a musing expression. He said absently, "Reckon we're even, Johnny boy. I saved you from Joe Lidski, you saved me from this piece of buzzard meat."

Laramie stood up and took the gun from Candy's unresisting hand. He said, "But why did you kill him? At least before we got the whole story?"

"I heard enough. The so-and-so said Colton's put a price on my head, didn't he? That's all I needed to know!"

"But I wanted him alive to talk to someone, the Army commander."

"We don't need him. I know enough. I know about the holdup planned for the morning." He glanced at Laramie, his face set in anger, looking years older suddenly. "I may be a thief, I may be a killer, I may be many things, but one thing I'm not. I'm not a traitor to my country!"

Laramie Nelson took Candy to the office of the Army commander, Lieutenant Colonel E. B. Coffrett, in the temporary barracks.

Colonel Coffrett was a bulldog of a man, short, stocky,

183

with gray, wiry hair and a permanent expression of distaste, a parade ground bark to his voice.

Also in the office was his adjutant, a Captain Moore. Laramie had heard of Moore, a handsome, dashing officer with a reputation as a ladies man. But he was much more than that. Laramie knew of his fine Army record, and he also knew that Moore had, at the amazing age of twenty-five, written a book on railroad military tactics which was a textbook used in many military academies, including West Point.

Laramie showed the two officers his credentials and quickly explained the situation as he knew it, mentioning that his mission was on the behalf of President Grant. Colonel Coffrett was impressed by this fact, and he was both astonished and offended by the mere idea of Nat Colton's scheme.

He got up from behind his desk and began to pace, short legs hitting the floor like stumps. "Take over the state! We have just fought a war over secession, sir!"

"I know that, Colonel. And Colton's making use of that fact. Most of his men are ex-Confederate soldiers."

"I find this hard to accept, sir, that any man would have the gall to attempt such a thing right under my nose! I will smash him, sir, smash him!" He smacked a fist into his palm.

"Colonel," Captain Moore interjected smoothly, "I believe the most immediate thing is the planned robbery."

"Quite right, Captain, quite right."

Colonel Coffrett wheeled and began barking questions at Candy Kesson.

They quickly learned the essentials of the robbery plan. Candy's men were to ambush the gold train about five miles from Carson City, in a narrow gorge. The track would be blown up with dynamite just before the locomotive reached the end of the gorge. Then Candy's men would deal with any troops on the train while the gold was being transferred to wagons and hauled away. It sounded simple and effective.

Colonel Coffrett leveled a finger at Candy. "I'm not a fool, sir! My men are patrolling the tracks to guard against just this very thing."

Candy blinked. "What thing?"

"Blowing up the tracks. How do you propose to get close enough to do that?"

"Oh, that." Candy shrugged. "That was figgered out weeks ago, when we first learned the shipment was going by railroad. The track was mined and the fuses buried. They lead a hundred yards away from the tracks. Your patrols will never discover the fuses."

"It can be done," Captain Moore said thoughtfully. "That method was used at Petersburg shortly before the capture of Richmond. Powder was exploded from a distance by the careful use of fuses. To my knowledge, that was the first time it was ever done."

The Colonel paced, scowling fiercely. Laramie saw now what Allison had meant; Colonel Coffrett wasn't the most intelligent man the Army could have had in charge.

After a respectful silence, Captain Moore said, "Sir, we could concentrate troops on the gorge, a sortie to capture the bandits before they light the fuses."

Colonel Coffrett stared at his adjutant through narrowed eyes. Then he snapped his fingers.

"Captain Moore, you will send a detail of men into that gorge. They will arrive at first light and engage the dynamiters."

"Yes, sir," Captain Moore, clicking his heels. His

glance met Laramie's, and Laramie Nelson was sure he detected sardonic amusement in the officer's eyes.

"I think Colton may take Candy's place," Laramie said, "since he no longer trusts him, may even think he's dead. He could even use his Regulators, as well as the outlaws."

"A ragtag bunch!" the colonel barked. "They'll stand no chance against regular troops!"

Laramie wasn't so sure, but he didn't think it would be diplomatic to say so. Instead he said, "Might I suggest something, Colonel? It might not be a bad idea to get off a wire to Carson, saying the Candy Kid is dead. That way, Colton is sure to lead the raid."

The colonel stared, then snapped his fingers. "Good thinking, Nelson. Good thinking indeed!"

Laramie glanced over at Candy. "And maybe we should take Candy along on the train. Just in case."

"Glad to oblige, Johnny boy." Candy grinned for the first time, a vicious, killing grin. "All I ask is first crack at Colton."

He was interrupted by a knock on the door. A trooper stuck his head in. "A man here to see you, Colonel sir."

Fred Royal was ushered in. He stopped short at the sight of Laramie. "Nelson! I didn't know you'd be here but I'm glad you are." Royal was unshaven, his clothes rumpled, his face gaunted. "I discovered last night that you were telling me the truth. My wife—" He paused, looking stricken. Then he squared his shoulders and went on.

"In a moment of anger with me last night, my wife revealed to me that all you told me is true. Colton boasted to her about it. He has some Napoleonic scheme of becoming Emperor of Nevada. My wife sides with him. I

186

have no apologies for my wife, gentlemen. She has never liked this country and my position here. It seems even my being governor wouldn't be—" His voice trailed off, and he looked at the colonel.

"That's why I'm here. Colonel. I'm resigning from the governor's race, but first something must be done about Nat Colton."

"And by God, sir, something will be!" Colonel Coffrett barked. "I will see this traitor hanged!"

"But first the gold shipment, sir," Captain Moore reminded him gently.

The colonel batted a hand. "Yes, yes, of course."

'Then I take it Colton knows his game is up?" Laramie asked Royal.

"I'm afraid so, Mr. Nelson," Royal said heavily. "My wife will have told him by this time."

"Which means Colton will certainly be leading the attack, probably with some, if not all, of his Regulators. He has nothing to lose now, and he'll hope to grab the gold and run with it."

The gold shipment was due to leave Virginia City shortly before noon the next morning. Laramie Nelson stood at the rear of the four-car train with Candy Kesson, watching the troops board. Candy's gun had been returned to him. It hadn't been decided what charges would be lodged against him. Robbery, followed by a prison sentence, was the most likely. No one seemed concerned about the death of Snake Fisher.

Captain Moore approached them. "We'll be pulling out in a couple minutes, Mr. Nelson. We've placed fifty men on the train. Another troop has been sent to the gorge. That should have that cleaned up long before we get there."

"Candy says he turned all the gold over to Colton, Captain. He's the only one knows where it is, what's left of it. It's important we take him alive. Otherwise, we may never find the gold."

The adjutant nodded his handsome head. "Those orders have already been issued, sir."

"Them orders mean nothing to me," Candy said flatly. "Not if I get Colton in my sights!"

"You kill him, Candy, and you'll have me to answer to," Laramie said.

Candy merely shrugged, turning away.

Laramie debated taking the youth's gun, but things might get hectic when Colton and his men hit the train. Unarmed, Candy wouldn't stand a chance.

They received the signal to board. The engine had steam up, puffing nervously. The gold was aboard, and the troopers had been dispersed along the train. Colonel Coffrett came aboard with Fred Royal, a signal was given, and they moved out jerkily.

Colonel Coffrett summoned Laramie to the first car, which he had taken over as his command headquarters. Royal was shaven and had changed into fresh clothes, but he still looked haggard.

"Well, we're prepared for them, Mr. Nelson," Colonel Coffrett said expansively. "I've a number of ex-Indian fighters in my command, you know. They'll have crept up on those dynamiters by now, I expect, and have them in custody."

"Along with the wagons," Captain Moore said.

"I've also wired east," the colonel said. "There'll be a

188

full regiment in Carson within a matter of days, sir, to deal with that rag-tag bunch of Colton's."

Laramie didn't feel nearly so confident, but he felt bound to compliment the officer on his thoroughness.

Colonel Coffrett preened. "I hope you will mention this to President Grant in your report." He laughed heartily. "A good word on high never hurts, eh?"

An orderly brought refreshments, whiskey was served, and time passed quickly, pleasantly. The sound of the wheels clacking on the rails, the puffing engine, the liquor and food... all had a lulling effect.

Laramie had to fight to stay awake, and he was slightly surprised when an officer entered the command car to announce that the gorge was just ahead.

Colonel Coffrett jumped up with a pleased smile, slapping the holstered pistol at his side. Laramie went to the front of the car with him. In a moment the colonel pointed to a guidon carried by a mounted trooper off to the right of the tracks. The trooper dipped it three times.

"That's the signal, sir." Colonel Coffrett said with satisfaction. "They've got the powder and the wagons." He cast a sidelong look at Laramie. "There's your plot, sir. All neatly tied up."

The engine didn't stop, but chugged on through the canyon rhythmically, steadily. Everyone relaxed; there would be no gold raid. Colonel Coffrett proposed a toast.

Three miles beyond the gorge they came round a bend and faced an oncoming train engine, pulling two cars.

At the same time dynamite sticks were tossed at the gold train from the ground, exploding and ripping the last car apart. The train screeched to a shuddering stop. There was instant pandemonium.

Laramie, thrown to the floor by the grinding,

screeching halt, clambered to his feet. His ears were assailed by a fusillade of shots, yells and conflicting orders. The troopers were completely disorganized, most of them having already stacked their weapons. Sergeants bawled, trying to sort them out and get them to the windows with their carbines. From somewhere a bugle sounded, thin and piercing above the thunderous noise of scattered gunfire.

Colonel Coffrett, Laramie saw, had been knocked out by the sudden halt. Two men were trying to revive him. Captain Moore took charge. Seemingly undaunted by the sudden attack, he was brilliantly organizing a defense, slowly bringing order out of chaos. Laramie realized that the man's reputation as a student of train warfare was well-deserved.

Seeing he wasn't needed, Laramie made his way, pushing and shoving, to the rear door. Gun in hand, he jumped across to the next car, snapping off a shot at a horseman who shouted at him. The man's shot ripped wood off the car just above Laramie's head. Then he was in the car and racing toward the rear.

All around him the troopers were settling down to work, firing back at the raiders now riding up and down the stalled train on both sides. It was something like being inside a boiler factory. The continuous roll of carbine fire was thunderous, and acrid smoke stung Laramie's eyes.

The last car was completely demolished. Laramie frowned at the wreckage and at the track, which seemed undamaged, then made his way back to the command car. The colonel was conscious, but he seemed dazed. Captain Moore had restored order, and his troopers were coolly returning the fire from outside.

Laramie yelled in his ear, "If we can back the engine, push the wrecked car off the tracks, then we can back into the gorge. The troopers back there can help us."

Captain Moore nodded. "We're holding them, but that's a sound idea. See if you can get to the engine."

Laramie made his way forward, clambering over the stacks of wood in the wood-car. Two troopers were firing steadily from the engine compartment. The fireman was down, huddled in death. The engineer was frightened but unhurt.

"Back the train," Laramie yelled at him.

The engineer stared at him without comprehension.

Laramie shook him by the shoulder. "We're going to shove the wrecked car off the tracks and back to the gorge!"

The engineer nodded, then gestured to the dead fireman.

"I'll fire it!" Laramie shouted.

He leaped up onto the wood car and started throwing wood down. Then he froze, staring. Two cars back was Candy Kesson, balancing delicately on the top of the car. He was looking past Laramie. Laramie glanced back toward the other engine. Nat Colton, at the head of a dozen mounted men, was loping toward them.

Candy, drawing his pistol, was still coming. Laramie scrambled for the top of the next car, shouting, "No, Kid, no!"

Just as Laramie reached the top, the engineer started the train backing, reversing the wheels, and Laramie had to grab at the boardwalk to keep from being thrown off.

He heard a shot. Candy had fired. Laramie risked a glance back and saw Colton still coming. The jerking train had spoiled Candy's aim.

Laramie stood up, drawing his Colt. "Don't do it, Kid!"

Candy glared at him, his face contorted. "Don't butt in, Nelson! Colton belongs to me!"

He started to bring his gun around, and Laramie fired carefully. Laramie saw dust puff up as his shot hit Candy's left shoulder. The shattering impact sent Candy tumbling from the slow-moving train, and he disappeared from sight. Laramie hoped he'd be picked up real soon with the rest of the wounded. He liked the Candy Kid.

Remembering, Laramie spun around in a crouch.

Colton had seen him and yelled something. He rode straight for the train, firing as he came. His shots went wild as the train continued to move. Laramie fell to one knee and took careful aim. He only wanted to wound, not kill. He squeezed off a shot, missed, then fired again. His second shot hit Colton, knocking him from the saddle.

Without hesitation Laramie leaped from the train. He landed on his feet, took a few stumbling steps and fell, rolling down the shallow embankment. He was on his feet immediately. Several of the raiders milled around their fallen leader.

Laramie started toward them, then slowed. It would be foolhardy to take on a dozen men.

Then he heard a fresh burst of gunfire. He glanced around. A group of mounted men were pounding down the track toward the train, firing as they came. The troopers from the gorge.

At this appearance of reinforcements, their leader on the ground, the raiders began to disperse, fleeing in all directions. Within seconds Nat Colton was all alone.

It was all over.

Laramie walked over to him. He wasn't dead, a wound seeping blood high on his shoulder. Moaning in pain. Colton was no longer a threat.

Holstering his Colt, Laramie glanced toward the train. It was slowing to a stop. He saw Captain Moore jump to the ground and hurry toward him. The mounted troopers had reached the train now and were scattering in pursuit of the fleeing raiders.

An hour later the gold train chugged into Carson City, the other train manned by troopers and backing in before it. The wounded Nat Colton had been questioned thoroughly by Fred Royal, in between blustering threats of hanging from Colonel Coffrett, and had revealed the hiding place of what gold was left from the two previous robberies. Royal was morosely happy with the smashing of Colton's plans, but he still remained firm in his intention of withdrawing from the governor's race.

The first person Laramie saw in the Carson station as he stepped off the train was Brock Peters, edging toward him through the waiting crowd, bowler hat bobbing.

As the Pinkerton man reached him, Laramie said, "Good news, Brock! It's all finished. You can wire President—"

"Never mind all that!" Peters snarled, waving a telegram at Laramie. "I want to know what this is all about! Five hundred dollars, indeed! Just what the devil do you think I am, a New York banker?"

Laramie Nelson stared at him, nonplused. And then, suddenly he started to laugh. A minute later he was loping toward his horse. "Excuse me, Breck. I'll see you soon. I've got to look for a good friend of mine. I had to shoot him!"